The Voice

A Novel

by

Maurice E. Kennedy, Jr.

THE VOICE

iUniverse books may be ordered through booksellers or by contacting:

iUniverse
1663 Liberty Drive
Bloomington, IN 47403
www.iuniverse.com
1-800-Authors (1-800-288-4677)

ISBN: 978-1-5320-5959-9 (sc)
ISBN: 978-1-5320-5960-5 (hc)
ISBN: 978-1-5320-5958-2 (e)

Library of Congress Control Number: 2018913939

Print information available on the last page.

iUniverse rev. date: 12/07/2018

Phase 1
The Abductions

Chapter 1

Melissa

9:15 a.m.

She was running a little late this morning, but it was okay. Darien would cover for her until she got there, just as he always did on Tuesdays. He was such a good friend. As she drove down the winding curves of Lake Shore Drive toward Metropolitan Central, there was a touch of sadness in her heart. Today was Michael's first recital, and she couldn't be there.

He seemed so happy, no sign of nervousness, not even for a six-year-old. He was solid as a rock, just like his father. He would have been so proud of him. If only he could see him now, all decked out in his rented tux, smiling—a pure bundle of joy eager and ready to leave his impression upon the world. Michael had shown signs of musical prowess at the early age of three, always singing or humming in perfect harmony to music on the radio, tapping his feet and clapping in perfect rhythm.

It was always so easy to pick out toys for him. Anything that made musical sounds, that had bells or jingles—toy pianos, even drums. He was always so happy with whatever Melissa bought for him. He would always smile and utter happy little sighs of glee. His musical spirit was passed down to him from his father. Stephen could play almost anything. Melissa met him in college when they were both students at Chicago University, he a senior, she a sophomore.

It haunts her like a dream; she remembers every detail so clearly. That cool, fresh spring breeze on that Wednesday morning when she saw him sitting on the campus lawn playing his guitar, singing a Billy Joel tune, smiling. She had just taken her biology midterm, and although she knew she had aced it, the relief from the pressure-filled atmosphere of the testing room had hit her like a brick when she finally got outdoors.

Stephen seemed to be there just for her, a kind of reward for the long hours of study, the "brain strain," the cramming, trying to maintain her 3.7 GPA. She had never seen him on campus before, never heard someone play so beautifully, so effortlessly. His talented expression seemed to beckon her over to him, so she went. She walked over, sat there on the grass in front of him, and just listened. He didn't pretend not to notice her; rather, he looked up at her, smiled, and just kept on playing, singing:

Honesty is such a lonely word.
Everyone is so untrue.

Honesty is hardly ever heard—
Mostly what I need from you.

Melissa was mesmerized. He was a handsome, clean-cut young man with locks of curly dark hair and a muscular build. He wore a T-shirt that read *Jimmy Hendrix Forever* under a picture of the guitar legend, who was playing his instrument with his teeth. A pair of faded blue jean shorts exposed his gorgeous legs, and his feet were relaxing in a pair of faded brown opened-toed leather sandals. After the tune, he introduced himself and asked her whether she had caught the wrong chord he had played back in the second stanza.

Melissa laughed at the obvious idiocy of the question and told him that he sounded great. They had lunch, walked around the campus, and began what turned out to be a beautiful relationship. A year later, they were married, and Melissa found herself with child, with Michael. She couldn't have been happier. They couldn't have been happier. After graduating, taking a daytime office job, and moonlighting as a Rite Aid security guard, Stephen was adamant about Melissa taking a year off to be home with Michael in his first year.

He knew that with his wife's diligence and tenacity as a student, Melissa would have no trouble bouncing back and picking up where she had left off, once Michael was one. He wanted his son to spend the first year of his life with his mother, not with a host of relatives, nannies, and babysitters. Melissa was reluctant at first, but eventually she listened to her man, the only man she ever truly loved, and succumbed to his request. All her life, Melissa had been a go-getter, a fiery, headstrong, determined lass who made her own decisions, never looked back, and never second-guessed herself.

Her determination and burning desire to not only succeed but also be the best at whatever she did had earned her near straight A's throughout her educational journey. She was always in the 5th percentile of her elementary, middle, high school, and college classes. As her high school valedictorian, she received a full four-year academic scholarship to the prestigious Chicago University. In her sophomore year, she secured a spot on the dean's list.

This was the culmination of a lifelong string of educational honors and achievements. She was no child prodigy, not in any sense whatsoever. She just worked hard all the time. Her passion for knowledge was surpassed only by her loving nature, subtle beauty, and burning desire to save all the children of the world from disease and illness, eliminating their pain and suffering—first as a registered nurse working in a children's clinic, then as a pediatrician, and finally as a researcher working on a team with other doctors and scientists, searching for cures.

Taking a year or so off from school, from her quest,

in order to raise her son, was a difficult decision. As it turned out, it proved to be one of the best things that could have happened to her, Michael, and Stephen. In that time frame, she bonded with Michael so deeply and so truly, blending with his essence. They became kindred spirits, much closer than the normal bond between a mother and her son. It only further fueled her desire to become a part of the salvation of every child she could, so that each and every one of them could live the life of love that she and Stephen were sharing with Michael.

Stephen was so wonderfully supportive. He was there for them in every way, in any way he could be, always making sacrifices and reassuring Melissa that he would never let the book close on her dreams. He was the very best.

His tragic death in a fatal car accident just one week before Michael's first birthday almost destroyed her. There was no way she could have survived and moved on if it hadn't been for Michael. It was as if Stephen lived on through him.

It was much more than just the normal father-and-son connection. At times when Melissa needed it most, those moments when she was at her lowest, Stephen would reach out and comfort his beloved Melissa through his son. She would actually sense his presence soothing her, helping her to heal, to regain her strength and eventually move on. As much as Michael needed Melissa for his survival, Melissa needed her son. After Stephen's death, Michael became her strength, her solace, and the reason she existed.

She had to be the best for herself so that she could do the best for him. So she needed to be, and so she was. She was there for everything, always ... except for today. Mrs. Neely, his piano teacher, would be there, as would his grandparents, his aunt Toni, and cousin Larry—but not her.

9:32 a.m.

As she rounded the corner of Seventh Avenue and pulled into the parking garage at the base of the hospital, she thought of what Mrs. Neely had shared with her earlier when she dropped Michael off. She said that Michael was by far the most gifted child she'd ever had the pleasure of training. She said that his ability to catch on so quickly, learning notes, scales, chords, and songs with the greatest of ease, was somewhat uncanny and that the joy he had in playing the piano seemed somewhat eerie.

To be a part of his school's talent show in the second grade as the most anticipated performer was one thing, but to be playing the first movement of Beethoven's Sonata in C# Minor, opus 27, *Moonlight* Sonata, after studying it for only three months and mastering it, was completely another.

Alicyn Davis, who was scheduled for surgery today to remove some lymph nodes from her abdominal region and chest cavity as part of her treatment for second-stage non-Hodgkin's lymphoma, needed Melissa today more than Michael did. Her condition had been misdiagnosed as mononucleosis at a neighborhood health clinic. After two weeks, the prescribed treatment failed to make the hardening lump on her neck go away. By the time a biopsy at Metropolitan had exposed the cancer, it had already begun to spread throughout her body.

Nothing on Earth could stop Melissa from being there to comfort Alicyn before she went into surgery. She had to reassure her that everything was going to be all right. Melissa's had to be the first face Alicyn saw when she came around after the successful operation.

At thirteen, Alicyn demonstrated an advanced sense of calm and understanding of her condition, even more so than her parents and younger sisters, who were always crying and upset. But Melissa knew just how scared Alicyn really was and vowed to help her 'pull through'. She knew that Michael would understand, and he did.

When Melissa explained to Michael why she couldn't be at his recital (she always explained everything to him), he said to her:

> Mommy, I'm going to do my best to play my song really good for Alicyn. Can Mrs. Neely tape it and play it for her to make her feel better after her operation?

When Michael said that, Melissa grabbed her son, pulling him tightly to her bosom, hugging him so that he would not see her crying, and whispered in his ear:

> Yes, honey, Mrs. Neely surely can and will. I'll be sure to tell Alicyn that a special treat will be waiting for her, to help her get better. So, do your best, baby, and always remember that Mommy loves you and that Daddy is watching you from heaven, okay?

That moment was just one of those special times when Michael would say or do something that would totally blow her away. Ever since he was a toddler, Michael was a quiet child with kind and gentle ways, never sassing, getting into trouble, or doing anything out of line. These qualities and more made Melissa realize just how special he was.

Even before Stephen's death, she knew that it was a blessing to have him and that the Lord had a special purpose for her son. She knew with every ounce of her being that it was her duty, responsibility, and honor to guide him in whatever path was chosen for him.

9:45 a.m.

Darien greeted Melissa at the nurses' station in his usual way of looking at his watch as if to scold her for her tardiness. Then he hugged and kissed her before giving up the lowdown on what was happening.

She and Darien got along well as the *low* people on the totem pole, the *new kids on the block.* Melissa knew that his interest in the well-being of the children under their care was genuine and sincere; she could feel it. From this, they developed a special bond instantly from day one. From that moment forward, they were in tune with each other's feelings and always had each other's back.

So, when Darien noticed Melissa's sad demeanor, which was in stark contrast to her usual bubbly, cheery self, he had to ask her what was wrong. The children, the doctors, the other nurses and assistants, everyone in the ward fed off her positive energy, which was amazingly consistent despite the death and despair that surrounded them. The thought that something could exist that was terrible enough to break Melissa's composure and spirit scared him.

Melissa:

> Michael's first recital is today, and I can't be there. He understands why—I talked to him—but still, I know he wants me there, and I'm kind of sad that I'm going to miss it. That boy is so special.

A sigh of relief escaped from Darien.

Darien:

> That, I can handle; anything else would have been a true disaster. Dr. Williams and the crew will be here around a quarter after to talk to Alicyn and her family. She's doing okay, but you know she's waiting to see you. She didn't get much sleep last night, and I couldn't give her a sedative. That's a strong little girl. I really hope that she'll be okay.

Melissa:

> Yeah, I know what you mean. Even if she pulls through okay, the postoperative prognosis includes months of radiotherapy. Chemo is out. Her parents were convinced that the possible long-term effects were too risky. She'll probably have to stay here for a couple of months before they let her go home and come in for outpatient treatments.

Darien:

> You know, Steven Jenkins was saying that there might be some openings at the Sea Shore House for her and her parents to take advantage of after surgery. I'll have to check with him and see if he can inform the goon squad before they chat with her folks. I'll stop and see him on my way out.

Melissa:

How's the rest of the crew? Are my babies okay?

Darien:

Yeah, the usual. Sandra started her treatments this morning and hasn't thrown up yet, which is good. She's been a little dizzy, so check on her a couple of times before lunch. Last night after dinner, we took everyone down to the playhouse. They had clowns and face painting, the whole nine yards. Everyone had a great time. Shannon even let them have Happy Meal snacks when we came back up.

Melissa:

That's a switch.

Darien:

Ain't that the truth. Usually she's such an asshole. I think some of your charm is rubbing off on her. She even let them watch *Nemo* while eating their snacks. Okay, honey, I'm outta here. The charts are updated. The meds are in the fridge and labeled. Catch you later, baby. Kiss Alicyn for me. I'll have Steven call you first thing.

Melissa:

Thanks, drive safely, get some rest.

9:50 a.m.

As Darien grabbed his bag and got on the elevator, Melissa paused to reflect on what a true blessing his friendship was. He helped to make this often taxing, traumatic ward bearable. As pleasant and uplifting as Melissa was, when things got tough, it was Darien who got to see her dark side. He was the only person there who saw Melissa weak, vulnerable, devastated, burnt out, and on the verge of losing it. She trusted him completely, which allowed for them to heal together.

At Metropolitan, children were diagnosed with many different kinds of cancer every day. The survivors, the ones who *pulled through,* were few compared to the number of little souls who made their trip to heaven on an almost daily basis. After Melissa comforted families before and after a death, Darien was there to comfort Melissa. Each child broke down a little piece of her through their suffering. As much as she was committed to her quest, sometimes she wondered if she could do it. It hurt her so much to see them in such pain.

To see the terrified looks in their eyes and in their parents' eyes as the doctors tried to *explain* the probability of *pulling through*. How does one tell a child, so full of hope and wonder and with so much yet to experience in life, that they are going to die?

You don't.

But as medical professionals, specialists in the field of cancer research and treatment, you know with more than a reasonable degree of certainty that they are. How does one convey the concept of a spreading malignant tumor, that despite the best treatment options available, continues to spread and will eventually cause vital organs to cease to function, leading to death?

You can't.

All we can do, the doctors, nurses, hospitals and research teams is whatever we can, whatever we must, to ease the suffering of those we can't save and to save the ones that we can. And somewhere in the midst, try to make some sense of this painful reality. These children are not stricken by way of years of neglect and substance abuse, as is the case of most of their adult counterparts, yet they have been selected by nature to play this part, which we are currently powerless to prevent.

Darien shared Melissa's thoughts and feelings. This she knew because they talked often, every day. Although his quest was somewhat different from her own in that he had no desire to become a doctor, they became good friends. As she turned to begin her rounds and prepare Alicyn for her ordeal, there was no way she could have known that she would never see Darien again.

11:15 a.m.

Mrs. Neely called the hospital to tell Melissa about the talent show. Mrs. Brady said that Melissa wasn't available but that she would give her the message. The recital went well. Michael was superb, as expected. He received a standing ovation that lasted over three minutes. As promised, Mrs. Neely taped his performance to play back for Melissa and Alicyn later.

Melissa was in Alicyn's room sitting next to her bed. The doctors had spoken with Alicyn's parents about an hour earlier. After the *goon squad* finished, she escorted the parents down to the intensive care unit outside of the OR. There, they would wait on pins and needles for a miracle, for their precious little girl to *pull through.*

Alicyn:

> When I come out, are you going to be there waiting for me?

Melissa:

> You bet, kiddo. I'll be sitting right there when you open those big, pretty eyes. So will your mom and dad.

Alicyn smiled as Melissa ruffled her long, pretty auburn hair, which she would lose in a month or so as a side effect from the radiation treatments. She firmly coupled Alicyn's hands in her own.

Alicyn:

> Will it hurt? How long is it going to take? Am I going to be sleepin the whole time?

Melissa saw the troubled look on her face, noticed the tears swelling up in her eyes, and felt the ripples as her little body began to shake. Her composure was beginning to crumble, and fear was entering into its place. Alicyn was a frightened little girl, after all. Melissa's armor kicked in, and she presented the stoic protector persona that Alicyn needed.

Melissa:

> I don't know, baby. The doctors need to take their time and get everything right so that you can be all better. But don't you worry, sweetheart; you'll be fast asleep the whole time, and you won't feel a thing. You'll be dreaming about Dora and Boots, and before you know it, it'll be all over. Then, your mom and dad won't be crying anymore.

Alicyn:

> My mom and dad are scaredy-cats. They're always cryin'. I'm the one who's supposed to be cryin'.

Melissa:

> It's okay for them to cry, honey. They're just crying because they love you and miss you. They can't wait until this is all over, so they can have you home again.

Alicyn:

> I know. I bet my stupid sisters have been all in my stuff, wearin' my clothes and everything. I can't never have nuthin to myself.

Melissa:

> They miss you too, baby. You just get some rest and stop thinking about all of that. You have to save your strength. Your body needs to get ready, okay? I'll be back to go down with you. Just lie back, close your eyes, and rest.

Kissing her on the cheek, Melissa squeezed Alicyn's hands, covered her up, then got up and left. On her way out, she glanced at the clock, dimmed the lights, and pulled the room door to, leaving it slightly ajar.

As she arrived back at the nurses' station, Mrs. Brady gave her the message from Mrs. Neely. Melissa smiled as she read the note. She thanked G-d for Mrs. Neely, who was much more than just Michael's piano teacher.

Melissa didn't want to call Michael until after she got off work. Alicyn's surgery was all she could think about. Her chances of *pulling through* were higher than normal, even for second-stage non-Hodgkin's lymphoma.

The surgeons at Metropolitan were the best in the business, but Melissa knew the risks of such a major operation and was still afraid for her.

11:30 a.m.

Melissa had just enough time to grab something to eat and relax a bit before they came for Alicyn. She had been running all morning and was a little beat. Darien had told her that adding a vitamin supplement to her diet would help give her more sorely needed energy, and she was beginning to realize that he was right.

After lunch, Melissa checked in on Sandra again, who was sleeping peacefully. Then she headed back to Alicyn's room. They would be coming for her soon, and she wanted to be there when they did, just like she was for all the children scheduled for surgery in her ward, on her shift.

11:50 a.m.

The trip to the OR was relatively uneventful. Alicyn was pretty calm. She didn't talk much; she just held Melissa's hand and seemed to be engrossed in her own thoughts.

Melissa knew that she was afraid, but Melissa's own anxiety over the pending surgery was magnified twenty times higher than Alicyn's, though she could never show it. She had to always be the rock, the comforter, and it tore her up inside. Only Darien knew her true pain. Only Michael. Never the children ... Never.

As she waited for the results, sitting off and on with Alicyn's parents in between her duties—visiting the other children, giving meds, and updating charts—Melissa's thoughts turned to little Donald, who was released just last week after being given an 85 percent chance of full recovery, pending his radiotherapy.

Everyone was so happy. They threw him a big party. Thinking of the sheer joy on his face as he was getting in the car to go home, after spending over eight months here at Metropolitan, made her smile inside.

It was reflections like this that made Melissa realize that this she was indulged her true calling. For she knew that she had been there for him and his family. She helped to ease the suffering and pain. Little Donald would never forget her. For the rest of his life, Melissa would always hold a special place in his heart, as he would in hers.

Each child that she grew to love, the ones who *pulled through,* helped to fill the void left behind when the angels came and took her other babies, the ones who didn't make it. Melissa stayed in contact with all the families. She visited the children often in their homes. They were always happy to see her, and she needed to see them.

7:38 p.m.

Nothing could stop the tears from flowing as Melissa drove home that evening. No one saw her break down at the hospital. No one could; it was not her place, not her charge. But in the solitude of her Volvo as she winded through the traffic, hurrying home to Michael, to her solace, Melissa could cry.

Heavy, heart-wrenching sobs that rocked
her entire being, her very soul.

She had to get herself together before she got to Michael. He would be anxious to tell her about the recital, about how he played, wanting her to hear the tape Mrs. Neely had made for her, for Alicyn. She wanted to be in good spirits and not spoil his moment. She knew that in time she could explain and that he would understand, as he always did. She told him everything.

So, stop your crying, Melissa. Stop your crying. Straighten
up, get it together, and get ready to embrace your son.

Melissa pulled over to the side of the road for a minute to gather her composure. She turned the car off, reclined, closed her eyes, and sat in silence until the images of her sitting next to Alicyn in her room, before she went down to surgery, pushed backward, to be recalled at a later time.

Poor Alicyn.

Alicyn didn't make it. The final analysis was postoperative trauma that resulted in cardiac arrest. They tried but couldn't revive her. The disease didn't kill her; all the major cancerous lymph nodes were removed. The five-hour operation was a success. So why didn't she survive? Why did she have to die? It didn't matter. What did matter was that once again Melissa felt powerless. Yes, she was there to comfort everyone, as she was so good at doing. She knew that Darien would stay late tomorrow so that they could comfort each other, as they always did, but that wasn't the point.

The issue was broader. The question was when, when would they stop having to comfort each other over the suffering and death of helpless children stricken with deadly diseases? As she pondered this question, she clearly heard a Voice whisper in one ear and repeat in the other:

Soon, Melissa. Soon.

Not startled in the least by this apparent response to her question, Melissa accepted the Voice as a comfort. It was somewhat soothing and vaguely familiar. As she rounded the corner of Park Side Terrace Avenue, about two and a half miles from her apartment complex, she saw flashing red and blue lights up ahead. There was a slight mist from the fog coming off the lake, so it was difficult for her to make out exactly what was going on.

8:02 p.m.

As she neared, she saw that the lights were coming from a police car. Upon arriving at the scene where several cars were slowing down to gawk at what seemed to be a serious accident, Melissa was approached by an officer who motioned for her to roll down her window.

Officer:

> Ma'am, there's been an accident up ahead, and we're asking people to take a left here and go around. The ambulance is on its way, and we need the area to be as clear as possible to let them through.

Melissa:

> I'm a nurse at Metro-Central. What happened? Maybe I can help until the paramedics get here.

Officer:

> So far as we can tell, it appears that that tractor-trailer over there lost control and ran that SUV into the embankment. Probably hydroplaned on this slick surface because of the mist; sideswiped a woman and her little girl. Damned shame. I'm sure he didn't mean to hit 'em. The mom seems to be okay, but the little girl is still trapped in the jeep. She's pretty banged up. She might not make it.

Melissa immediately thought of Alicyn, who didn't *make it.* Melissa could still see Alicyn's face, her smile. She could still feel the silky smoothness of Alicyn's long, curly auburn hair between her fingers. The faint aroma of the Sweet Honesty that Alicyn wore all the time still tickled her nostrils. Melissa was not going to sit back and wait for another little girl to die. Powerless? Not this time.

Melissa:

> I have my bag in the trunk. Let me take a look at her. At best, I can administer proper first aid and give the paramedics a better assessment of her condition. It might help to save her life.

Officer: (agreeing)

> Okay, ma'am. It sure is a blessing in disguise that you came by when you did. Park your car over here, and I'll take you to her.

The officer told her to get her bag, and he would then take her to the scene. Melissa did as she was instructed, and the officer took her to the accident victims. As expected, the mother was hysterical, screaming and completely out of control.

Mother:

> My baby! Oh G-d, my baby! Somebody please help my baby!

Another officer was not doing very well in his attempt to restrain the distraught woman without further complicating any injuries she might have sustained. As Melissa approached the black Toyota Four-Runner and looked into the jeep, a cold chill crept into her spirit and over her soul.

The child, who looked to be about Alicyn's age, was still strapped in the front passenger seat, motionless and apparently unconscious. She observed that neither airbag had deployed, probably saving both of their lives.

The front passenger-side window was smashed due to a tree branch that had crashed through during impact, striking the little girl in the head. Auto glass was all over the seat and the little girl. Melissa could see that she was bleeding badly and rushed to her aid. She climbed into the jeep through the open driver's side door, checked the little girl's vitals, and carefully examined her for any obvious injuries.

She was alive—barely breathing but alive. Blood was flowing freely from a deep gash on the right side of the little girl's head, just above her jawbone, which was clearly broken. Using a scarf that Melissa had around her neck, she applied a facial tourniquet to control the bleeding.

She used a belt that the little girl had on to secure a makeshift brace to support her head and then carefully brushed the pieces of glass away. She climbed out of the jeep. She noticed a man watching her from a nearby car and motioned for him to get out and come help to remove the child from the vehicle.

The man, who was tall and appeared to be in his early fifties, wore glasses and had on a long trench coat. He responded quickly to her request. He had been watching carefully the whole time and realized that Melissa was trying to save the little girl. The officer who had brought Melissa to the victims went back to directing traffic, as he observed that she had things under control and now had some assistance.

When the man approached, Melissa instructed him to climb into the back seat of the jeep while she got into the front and unfastened the little girl's seat belt. Then together, they would gently angle her out of the jeep. There, Melissa could administer proper first aid and examine her more thoroughly before the ambulance arrived. The man nodded in agreement and watched as Melissa crawled back into the jeep.

After successfully unfastening the little girl's seat belt, Melissa turned to look in the back for the man to begin helping her ... He wasn't there.

At that moment, she felt the man grab her from behind and place a cloth with some kind of chemical on it over her mouth and nose, cutting off her breath. Melissa immediately tried to hold her breath, but it was too late; he had caught her with her mouth open.

Although she was an advanced martial arts student in tae kwon do, Melissa was powerless to do anything. She was in a closed space that restricted her movement. The man, who was amazingly strong, held her securely from behind and the chemical that was on the cloth was quickly knocking her out. As she began to lose consciousness, before she went completely under, Melissa heard the man whisper in her ear:

Soon, Melissa. Soon.

Then she blacked out.

8:27 p.m.

When the ambulance arrived, the mother and her little girl were standing next to the officers and the older man in the trench coat. Melissa lay unconscious by the side of the SUV wrapped up in a blanket.

Officer 1 to paramedic 1:

> We were able to get her out of the jeep. She doesn't appear to be hurt too bad, but we didn't think it was best to try and revive her.

Paramedic 1:

You did the right thing. What happened?

Mother:

We were following behind her when she suddenly lost control and smashed into the embankment. Probably hydroplaned on this slick surface because of the mist. I stopped and ran to see if I could help her, while my daughter used my cell phone to call the police.

Little girl:

I called 911. Is she dead?

Paramedic 2:

No, she's alive. I checked her vitals and for signs of any obvious injuries. She appears to be fine. She probably just passed out from shock.

Officer 2 to paramedic 2:

When we arrived, this gentleman helped my partner and I remove her from the jeep. She's a good driver. She just missed hitting that tree.

Paramedic 2:

You guys did just fine.

Officer 2 to the woman, child, and older man:

> We'll lead the ambulance. Please follow us to the hospital where we can get some more information.

8:43 p.m.

The paramedics lifted Melissa onto a stretcher after putting on an oxygen mask. Then they gently placed her into the back of the ambulance. After strapping her down securely, one paramedic went to the front and began to slowly drive off. As instructed, the woman with her daughter and the older gentleman followed. The officers led the whole entourage to a nearby hospital.

No one who knew Melissa ... ever saw her again.

Life

We are born into the human race
Unafraid and completely new
We exist to occupy time and space,
And we are loved by only a few ...

We open our eyes so that we may see
Our souls being stripped of pride
We cannot defend, and so we flee,
But there is nowhere for us to hide ...

We find a love and build a home
And reach for dreams that are within our mind
About this planet Earth we travel and roam,
There is no peace, and justice ... isn't blind

We see ourselves through surveys and polls
We know of the Lord and wonder why
We inscribe our lives in books and scrolls,
For we are born, only then to die

Chapter 1—Supplement

Michael

None of the music stores had any left. None of the radio stations had any to give away. There wouldn't be any scalpers hovering like vultures, seeking desperate patrons that evening who wouldn't hesitate for a moment to cough up double the ticket price for the sold-out concert. There were simply none to be found. If you didn't get your ticket within a week after they went on sale, then you blew it. That is of course unless you planned on hopping to the next city in two weeks, for the next show. His schedule was always listed online at *www.moonlight.com,* always accurate, always up to date. He would have it no other way.

Just before going solo, Michael DuPree changed his name to Michael Melissa Stephen, in honor of his father who perished in a fatal car accident just before he turned one, and his mother who disappeared in a cloud of mystery when he was six. He barely remembered his father. All he could muster were faint images and distant auras. Yet one would expect that the abrupt loss of the special bond he shared with his mother would have had an adverse effect on his development; it didn't; and if that were the case, no one would have ever been able to tell.

He was affectionately known as Maestro Michael by his comrades in the music business and his hundreds of thousands of fans, and he was in town this evening to assist the sunset in the closing of another day. At twenty-three, he was deemed the most gifted pianist of the modern era.

After turning pro at the tender age of sixteen and playing for years with the likes of the New York Philharmonic, the Philadelphia Orchestra, the Chicago Symphony Orchestra, and countless others, Michael decided to go solo and go on tour. He would finally get to live his dream of sharing his gift with the world.

When he was not wooing standing-room-only crowds in some concert or opera hall, he was serenading sick children and their families in some recovery house, pro bono of course. The children loved him, just like they loved his mother. At each recital, he always opened with Beethoven's *Moonlight* Sonata, just like he did at the age of six, during his musical debut as the star performer of the now legendary Woodrow Wilson elementary talent show. Nowadays, however, he played all three movements.

As it was, music was his only love, his only passion. Michael never married; he existed solely for his music. He wouldn't have been able to share his life, a major requirement in any successful marriage.

When he was not playing, he was studying. By the age of fifteen, Michael had mastered all the genres, including orchestral, opera, jazz, and R&B, but classical piano was his forte, and Beethoven was his specialty.

In concert, he was mystical. The sounds, the melodies, the movements, methods, and moods that emanated from Alicyn, his pearl-white Steinway baby grand, could melt anyone's heart. When people heard the maestro, they *felt* the maestro. To further enhance the experience, each recital was accompanied by a picture screen that showed his hands and fingers as they gracefully caressed the keyboard.

You can't believe it ... but you're there.
The lights dim ... the crowd noise fades
From an audible din
Into faint whispers
To a deadly silence.
The maestro appears on stage.
He glides to Alicyn ... takes his seat,
Then gently places his hands on the ivories.
For the next hour two hours ... no intermission.
The audience is seduced into tears.
As they listen, they undergo a magical metamorphosis
And are transformed into *Junkies for Michael,*
Forever.

Every time, at every recital, as he plays song after song, melody after melody the tears well up in his eyes. The source is a bottomless well of emotion that bubbles to the surface, overflowing, exploding, and releasing the pressure.

The deep sorrow that he feels for the loss of his kindred spirit, his Melissa, his mother ... is to the bone. It manifests itself as an overpowering surge of energy, a force that he conducts through his soul, his body, his arms, hands, fingers, and eventually into Alicyn.

He never tries to curtail its flow, for it is this power that is the very essence of his musical genius. It drives and sustains him. His mother, Mrs. Neely, if they could only see him now, all decked out in one of his exquisite, tailor-made black tuxes, a pure bundle of emotional energy, crying, playing, and mourning—and in the process, extending his musical legacy upon the world.

As he ends the concert
With a masterful rendition of Frédéric Chopin's
Ballade no. 1 in G Minor, op. 23,
The members of the audience, a motley crew
Spanning all ages, ethnic origins,
and social economic statuses,
They rise to their feet
And with a thunderous round of applause and whistles
Accompanied by wails of pure joy,
They drown out the Maestro's final
keystrokes and chords,
A tribute that lasts long after Michael has left the stage,
Over three minutes.
Another concert from the classical
pianist extraordinaire
Michael Melissa Stephen
Has ended.
... An era has begun ...

And the world will never be the same,
... Exuberantly changed ...
Forever.

Chapter 2

Celeste

Love Ballad #1

We had arrived there
            Tempted by desires and sensations
            Seduced by dreams and expectations
Embraced by two people who had become,
            Two lovers who were as one

We came to rest there
      Lost between hiding and seeking
      Torn between giving and keeping
Episodes between two people who had cried,
      But who had never really tried

We almost stopped there
      Trapped between fears and wishes
      Caught between anger and kisses
Memories between two people who were sure,
      That their illness had no cure

      From our hearts' passionate desire in the past
            To our love's burning fire at long last

We have since arrived here
    Secure amongst our relatives and friends
    Surviving amongst the losses and wins
Existing with our child who is grand,
    But who was never really planned

We can stay here
    Traveling at unprecedented speeds
    Satisfying our superficial needs
Survival between two people who now see,
    The path to their imminent destiny

We shall remain here
    Warm between laughter and sorrow
    Safe between today and tomorrow
Moments between two people who now know,
    You can only reap what you sow

The email from Capt. Williams was in her inbox when she signed on this morning: "Good morning, Celeste ... you've got mail." She hated that little jingle, but she couldn't figure out how to turn it off. (Sheila would've known.) Nevertheless, being the diligent worker that she was, she knew that *cyber-communo-techno-bullshit* was the hottest craze at the precinct. Everybody was into it, so she had to join the party.

Along with texting, social media, and selfies, it was all a bunch of malarkey according to her.

Gone were the good ole days when you simply picked up a damn telephone (*how be it a cell phone these days, not your standard run-of-the-mill land line or even the not so convenient telephone booth anymore*) and placed a call. No answer? Nobody home? Then just leave a message for them to call you back and possibly leave you a message. Nothing wrong with a little telephone tag.

One kinda of got used to checking phone messages. It sorta made you feel important to see the light on the answering machine letting you know that someone had called you. Someone actually took the time to pick up a phone, dial your number, listen to the rings, listen to your message saying that you weren't available, and then leave you a detailed message. She hardly ever got phone calls anymore, not even on her cell.

Celeste, yeah, you're an old fashioned kinda girl. The root of why you can't break free from Milton … can't think of that right now.

When, Celeste? When?

The Voice again. Always there. Always telling her to do the right thing and dump this creep, after a few more solid kicks in the balls. But the Voice never told her how to do it without shattering her world, the world she had built for herself, bit by bit, piece by piece. She needed help.

Celeste snapped back to reality, to the *tech-no* age, opened the email from Capt. Williams, and read it carefully. She almost peed on herself from excitement. G-d damn it, this was almost too good to be true. She read it three more times, printed it out, and then filed it away in her cabinet.

She didn't trust computers (primarily because she wasn't good with them). She was comfortable only with the things she knew, and what she did know, she knew well. She wanted to make sure that she secured the facts. She was not going to let anyone or anything screw this one up.

For all the assholes who got off on some technicality or because some poor, frightened victim, scared shitless of the possibility of retaliation, decided at the last moment not to press charges, this one (*oh yeah baby*) was in the bag. She knew that they had this sleaze ball by the nuts, and she was going to make sure that they squeezed real hard.

After speaking one final time with Angela, the eighteen-year-old victim, and checking one more time with the DA to be sure that she had his full support on this one, Celeste called over to the Thirty-Fifth Precinct to have Capt. Williams print (from the cyber files) two hard copies of the bad-boy Romero's rap sheet, along with this latest police report, seal up the package, and overnight it to her office. She told him to use FedEx just to be sure. No system glitches with records retrieval with this baby. They had caught a big break this time.

Romero (suspended driver's license from a previous DUI conviction) was pulled over for a moving violation last night. The plainclothes duo of Robertson and Smith had observed him swaying in and out of lanes on I-76 West last night, almost causing several accidents.

When the officers pulled up behind him with their flashing lights and instructed him via bullhorn to pull over, Romero continued to drive in the same reckless manner for about five miles.

Calling for backup, Sgt. Smith (who radioed, while detective Robertson continued to try and get Romero to pull over) received assistance from three cruisers and a paddy wagon. They followed him until there was little traffic, right at the I-476 overpass, where they finally had room enough to box him in and force him to stop.

Fortunately, he didn't make a run for it. No high-speed chase ensued, and no one got hurt ... not even Romero. Several of the assisting officers (guns drawn) approached his fire-red Trans Am.

Officer Smith *(using a bullhorn, calling for Romero to get out):*

> Exit the vehicle.
> Place your hands on top of your head.
> Step away from the vehicle.
> Turn around.
> Slowly walk backward toward the sound
> of my Voice.
> Stop. Drop to your knees.

In the blink of an eye, Romero was face down on the ground where he was cuffed and helped up, etc. etc. *(you know the drill, we've all seen the 'cop' shows)* There were no passengers in the car. Romero was taken into custody without incident.

In the car (phony registration, inspection, and emission stickers) under the driver's seat, they found a loaded .38 revolver (unlicensed) and an open forty-ounce bottle of Old English 800. Also in the car was $15,000 in cash in a brown paper bag, large quantities of marijuana, and some fifty or so individual packets of crack cocaine.

All packaged up and ready for sale with an estimated street value of about $20,000. Romero was drunk and later found to be under the influence of drugs ... a prime catch. There was enough here to lock this thug up where he belonged, for a very long time—not to mention poor Angela (silly girl).

Out at the club, hanging out, looking to have some fun like most young women from her hood, trying to find that right man whom she could "git wit" in her own way, in her own time, that could help her "make it" ... you know ... live the life ... make the scene, not realizing that she was going about it the wrong way, not fully understanding the danger she was putting herself in. Just like the naïve little lass in that Eagles song "Those Shoes":

You just want someone to talk to
They just wanna get their hands on you
You get whatever you choose
Oh no you can't do that

Once you started wearing those shoes ...

Angela just didn't see it coming.

Damn girl ... brother is fine
Check out the cuts
Check out the bling-bling
Let me give this man the eye
Let him know I'm lookin ...
Yeah girl

Oh, he was looking all right, but you would never know it. You see, Romero was smooth with his game. He would cruise the hottest clubs, looking for the *bangin babes,* the sexy, fly mamas who always had the sucker dudes ogling and pawing all over them.

Yeah man, he was cool. James Bond type all the way.

He'd walk in, check the place out (to make sure he didn't see anyone he knew) get his rum and Coke or piña colada and would then just scope. Never with a crew, always alone. Always dressed to show his muscular build, looking like LL Cool J but with more clothes on and in better taste.

Once he spotted a honey (a wannabe model, body ... but no brains on how to use it), he would just chill in her area. Not too close though, just far enough away to be noticed. Bobbing his head to the beat, never dancing, just cooling out. But definitely within her eyesight. He would never look directly at her, just all around her ... at her girlfriends, not staring, just noticing them, smiling but never at her ... his objective ... his target ... his prey.

Yeah man, sweet.

Romero could almost taste her. Young brown sugar, sexy ... ready ... ripe. Like a piece of fruit at harvest. There for him. Waiting to be snatched up and devoured.

His libido was up, and his senses were tingling. He knew that this was the one. *Okay, man, let's go. Get ta steppin'.* Romero's trap was ready; it had been perfected over the last couple of years. It never failed, never faltered.

Just like Romero had a nose for soon-to-be victims like Angela, Celeste had a nose for the scum of the Earth like Romero. Angela was about to be caught.

So be it ... too bad, so sad.

Thank the Lord for Celeste. For Angela would be the last prize on his shelf, the epilogue to his sordid saga. If he was right about this being the one, he would know it soon enough. If not, he would move on to another part of the club and, if need be, eventually to another spot altogether. He had all night. Nowhere to go, nothing to do. He had made his quota for the night. He always made his quota.

Being in the game wasn't good enough for him; he *was* the game. The epitome of a good salesman, street dealer extraordinaire. Low-key, kept to himself ... a true loner. He knew how to pick his customers. Oh yeah ... he didn't just sell to anybody. His clients always had money to burn.

No strung-out crackheads who robbed, stole, gave up the goodies ... anything for a fix, for that next hit. Naw man, those roaches were nothing but trouble. Bad news waiting to happen. Cool Romero played it smart. He stayed away from anything and anybody that would bring down the heat or draw attention from the other street hustlers.

He was a ghost. Here today, gone tomorrow. The big-time pushers, the suppliers ... they loved him. Romero always paid on time, in full, and in cash. He kept extra dough around from his profits to help him pay off just in case he didn't unload all his stash.

Cool Romero never stacked more than he could handle. Sometimes a little more, sometimes a little less. Kept the suppliers guessing, moved around. They didn't mind; he always delivered. He rose quickly on the street, picked up a rep. No one messed with Romero; it was bad for business. He kept the underground economy flowing. If some dipshit crew plotted to move on him, you know, "stick him for his paper," word got out.

Let it be. Leave him alone.

Once, Romero got busted and went down for a two-year stretch. He did his beef, he didn't sing. They tried. No go. He was tight, held his own. When he got out, the word was already out. He could be trusted. So after a minute or two, he was back on the block in full effect. He had earned his autonomy and was left to do his own thing.

Keeping it tight in the big house had its rewards. Several of the big boys wanted to recruit him into their organizations' hierarchy and bring him on board to work exclusively for them. They wanted to promote him and move him up the chain. He respectfully declined.

They let him be. Romero needed to be a free spirit, a floater, because he had another agenda. He was a predator. Couldn't have no ties, folks couldn't know too much about him—where he was going, what he was doing tonight.

Naw, man, catch you later ... see you around.

He stayed clean and sharp, not flashy and pimped out. DKNY, not Versace. A red Trans Am, not a black Beamer.

Tims, yeah, man ... had to sport them trees you know, for the honeys.

But with Calvin Klein's, not Sean Jeans. Not everything he had on was Rocawear, just a few things. Romero hit the gym but not hard. Stayed in shape and kept a six-pack but didn't bulge through his clothes in the wrong places. Hustling on the street was a means to an end. Angela found out just what Romero was really about.

Pimping?

Naw, man, no time to keep track of no herd and all that.

Hustling?

Just a cover player, a way to make some quick cash.

This night was lucky for him. Romero only had to hit three clubs before he ran across the right chick. From the moment he spotted her and peeped her game, he felt that she would be easy pickings, and he was right. He had become good at the hunt. He knew his prey well. Angela was a fly eighteen-year-old bomb shell, built to the tee and as fine as she wanted to be. She dressed to entice, turning heads, breaking necks. The brothers she wanted to attract, who looked like Romero, wouldn't give her no play.

Angela looked too good, and they figured that she would be too hard to pull. They saw her flagging all the other dudes and left her alone.

Naw, baby, you ain't dissin' me in front of my homies.

The fly dudes went after the lowly, wannabe not-so-fly girls because they would be easier to score, especially around Angela. The other sisters loved it when the *banging* brothers gave the rap to them and not Angela. They knew that they couldn't touch her, but the brothers didn't want her; they wanted them.

The *bumy* dudes, the ordinary blokes came at Angela in droves. All night. Wave after wave. They just wanted to get close enough to smell her sweet perfume, (it had to be sweet, as good as she looked) maybe get a dance (fast ... never slow). Maybe get close enough to *cop a feel* and touch her silky, smooth skin. Hopefully some of their homeboys would see them talking to her, and then they could lie later and make up all kinds of bullshit stories.

Angela was getting tired and pissed off at this scenario that played itself out night after night, club after club. The girls loved having her around and flocked to wherever she was like rock-star groupies ... because she always drew the men (and the ladies too ... the ones on the other side of the game, if you know what I mean). All kinds, the right ones and the wrong ones. Romero was *very* wrong, but you would never know it. Always cool, a perfect gentleman, smooth and calculating.

After observing the scene and seeing that Angela was the right fish waiting to be caught, Romero made his move. Standing at an open bar table a few feet away, he caught the attention of one of her girlfriends who was more than too eager to come over to him when he beckoned.

He made sure that Angela saw this and made doubly sure not to make eye contact with her during this *setup stage*. He would then buy the other girl a drink or two, (never three), shoot the breeze, lay down a little rap, and appear genuinely interested in her.

Angela noticed this of course; she had been trying to get Romero's attention ever since she spotted him. (Careful what you wish for, young lady.) Inside, she was furious. Outside, she had to keep her cool.

Angela (thinking to herself):

How could a fly dude like that be interested in her? Look at her! Look at me! What's up?

Romero didn't prolong the charade for too long. He didn't want his prize to get up and walk away. He had to move quickly. He positioned himself between *girlie,* with his back toward Angela, so that she couldn't make out what he was about to say or see what he was about to do.

Romero (to one of Angela's Barbie dolls):

> Hey, babe, thanks for coming over and all, but I was checking out your girlfriend. The sweet sissta over there in the pink halter top and the jeans skirt. I saw that dude standing next to her and didn't know whether or not that was her man. You know, I didn't wanna step on his toes. I ain't that kinda dude.

Girlfriend:

> That ain't Angela's man.

Fool ... why did you say her name?

Girlfriend:

> He's just some guy sweatin' her. You wanna holler at her?

Girlfriends will be girlfriends, and even though she would have loved to have had Romero all to herself, she would rather see Romero with Angela than with some other chick. This way, they could *keep it on the block,* and Angela could tell the sisstas all about him later.

Dude is fine, girl. No threat.
Brother is smooth, girl, smellin' all good.
He's nice; he even bought me two drinks.

Romero:

> Hey, listen. When you go over there, keep it on the DL, you know? Don't broadcast all loud on me. I'm kinda on the shy side. Don't want too much attention.

Romero (taking her hand and slipping her a twenty-dollar bill):

> Between you and me. Cool?

Girlfriend:

> No problem, baby. You so sweet. Angela is a real nice girl. I know she looks fly and all that and got all those dudes hangin' around her. But trust me, she don't want none of them. Believe me, she'll be right over.

Girlfriend leaves to go and send Angela to her fate. Romero just plays it cool, sipping on his drink, checking out the sounds ... nowhere to go ... nothing to do. He's got all night. He strikes his best *GQ* pose, rehearsed many times over, and waits patiently. The snare has been sprung.

Girlfriend to Angela (in a hushed tone):

> Girl, you ain't gonna believe this. 'Don't look, don't look. That guy I was just talkin' to, he bought me two drinks.

She'll never tell Angela about the twenty dollars. All the other girlies will know (with the quickness) as soon as Angela walks over to him. It'll be their dirty little secret ... something to have over Angela.

Angela (obviously pissed):

> Yeah ... and?

Girlfriend:

> Wait, wait, check it out. He called me over because he thought that guy you were talking to was your man, girl!

Angela (shocked and in disbelief):

> What?

For a second, she glances over at Romero, who notices of course out of the corner of his eye.

Girlfriend:

> He wants to holler at you. Dude is fine.
> He's sweet, and he's a real gentleman ...
> girl. You better ease your little hot ass on
> over there and git them digits.

Angela is flattered and still in disbelief, but she knows not to blow this chance. She gets up, straightens her skirt, applies some lip gloss, arches her back, and struts her best step over to Romero.

Cut to the chase.

Romero is very charming, a perfect gentleman. They talk, they dance (fast and very slow), they laugh, and Angela feels like a queen for the rest of the night. He convinces her to tell the girls that he wants to go and get a bite to eat after the club, inviting them all to come ... his treat of course.

They follow Angela and Romero to the local after-hour's eatery. They dine, laugh some more, talk. It's all good. For the next week or so, Angela and Romero are a hot item. He's so fly and so nice ... so smooth. Angela is swept. Angela is hooked ... in more ways than she knows.

You see, this is all part of the game ... the trap. When the trap is sprung, there is no escape. When Romero decides to make his move, he is quick, decisive, and to the point. This whole *item thang* is only designed to last but for so long. A couple? Please ... only in her wildest dreams.

Once it's over, it's over.

The Voice …

Time to give it up, babe; you've been wined and dined long enough.

For most women, Romero's MO would be considered a player's dream—no harm, no foul. She got what she wanted; he's going to get what he wants. If she's *down wit the program,* then great. She'll enjoy it just as much and maybe even more than he will. For these sisters, the only scar is the complete disappearing act. No phone call, no text message, no sightings—nothing. Gone in a puff of smoke. Here tonight, gone in the morning for good.

Oh well, it was cool. I got with a fly dude. He showed me a real good time, bought me some nice things. We got busy once … real busy.

You see, Romero was an excellent lover, took his time, made her feel special, completely satisfied, the best that she ever had in her young life. *I wanted it; he wanted it. No harm, no foul.*

Cool Romero, stick and move, bun and run, hit it and done. Except for the ones (like poor Angela) who weren't *down wit the program.* Somehow in her young, confused mind, she knew that if she gave it up too soon, Romero would get ghost. She wanted the magic to last just a little bit longer, so she decided to make him wait … let him know that she was interested but not quite ready to go all the way yet.

Poor Angela. Wrong move … too bad, so sad.

This would be all right mentally for the normal dude. The normal dude would banter back and forth with a few head games, maybe even play the *well, nix you* role a little bit, but in the end, he'd stick around, for he knew that the prize was coming.

Such is the lot for most men. Angela was a beautiful young woman who would soon be his. *Just keep your cool, keep playing your cards right.* She'd give in ... give it up ... soon enough. Romero was far from normal.

This game was going to end tonight in one of two ways. One, the way most of them ended, which was in blissfully satisfying sex. Or two, the Angela way. The moment that Romero sensed that she wasn't *down wit the program,* he would just stop sweet-talking her and then coolly, calmly and collectively commence to beating the living crap out of her—punching, kicking, using his belt (he always had one on) or whatever else he could grab. No mercy, no reprise, no matter how much she begged, pleaded, or said that she would *do it.* Oh no, sister; it was too late for that. No rape beef here.

You see, Romero could take it either way. The sick, twisted bastard got just as much pleasure from the beat down as he did from the sex. It didn't matter. He never said a word, not until the very end when Angela was lying on the floor in a bloody pulp, almost unconscious:

Romero (whispering ever so softly in Angela's ear):

> If you ever tell anyone about this, sweetheart, about me, baby girl, then I'll find you, Angela, and I'll come back and finish the job.

Romero collected his things after taking one more hit, then tossed Angela a dime bag of weed. Smiling wickedly, he walked out the door, leaving it open:

> A little something extra to remember me by. Catch you at the club ... or not.

Celeste had an uncanny way of putting the pieces of unsolved cases together, like the other Angelas. She was very good at following her gut instincts to logical conclusions that eventually led to arrests and then to convictions with stiff sentences. Everyone respected and admired the passion and due diligence she exercised in catching creeps like Romero. She seemed to always find a way to get victims to press charges and testify.

Romero didn't force himself on any woman ... ever. All his sexual encounters were consensual. Celeste knew not to waste time with any kind of rape charge with him.

She had the bastard on everything else: possession with the intent to sell; driving with a suspended license; reckless endangerment (traffic); another DUI; phony registration and inspection; no insurance; weapons offenses; (no resisting arrest or assaulting a police officer though; that would have been grand); and of course, the icing on the cake, Angela ... who agreed to ID Romero in court as the *wanna be lover* who messed her up pretty bad.

Celeste was good. She was sharp. She worked her magic in the system, pulling out all the stops. She rose in the ranks quickly. With a bachelor's in criminal science from the University of Pennsylvania and a degree from the prestigious Temple University Beasley School of Law, she passed the bar on the first try, something that hadn't been accomplished in six years in any state.

After celebrating for just one week, Celeste didn't want to sign on with any of the many law firms that made her lucrative offers ... *no way Hosea.*

Celeste had a plan, just as calculating as Romero's, on track and on target—but for good intentions. Celeste took the exam to become a police officer and passed. She wanted to be a cop, and so she became. A rookie police officer with a juris doctorate? ... hmmmm ... that's interesting, kinda like in reverse, right? Celeste wanted to walk the beat on the *other* side of the street.

From running away from home to escape the physical (not sexual) abuse from her father, who also beat her mother and lone sibling on a regular basis, she learned the streets from the wrong perspective.

Her father tried to molest her once, but she fought him off at twelve ... cold-cocked him with a table lamp. He then proceeded to beat the shit out of her, but he never tried to touch her in that other way ever again. Her sister Sheila (two years her elder) wasn't so fortunate.

So, on the street now and again, tricking was never a viable option. The pimps tried to *recruit* her, but they too were unsuccessful. She survived anyway she could—little odd and end jobs here and there, running errands for people, stealing food, bagging at the grocery store, pumping gas ... whatever.

In the beginning, her mom worried about her, but when she found out that Celeste never missed one day of school, not one day, she began to accept that somehow the Lord had sent an angel to watch over her little girl and that it was better this way. At first, for a long while, Celeste hated her mother for not standing up to her father, for not protecting her and Sheila.

She couldn't understand how she could allow this sorry excuse for a man, for a human being, this animal, to get away with what he was doing to them.

But when she would run away, when she was gone for a few days, that hatred would turn to concern and eventually, pity. She worried about her mom and Sheila. They had found a way to deal with it, to internalize the pain and to accept the abuse as their fate. Celeste couldn't do it. She wasn't built like that, so she ran. Her only escape from the reality was not to live it.

She found solace in a little old lady named Ms. Sarah, whom she met at the market one afternoon after school. After bagging her groceries, Ms. Sarah asked Celeste if she would help her get them home. Ms. Sarah told Celeste that she lived a few blocks from the store and that she sometimes had trouble rolling her little shopping cart, which had a loose wheel.

Ms. Sarah:

> I'll give you a little something extra, honey. Be a dear and help little ole Ms. Sarah out.

Celeste did so and for the next ten years; Celeste helped little ole Ms. Sarah with the groceries. You see, Ms. Sarah had seen Celeste at the market on occasion and noticed her demeanor. In contrast to the other kids (all boys), she saw that Celeste was quiet, not aggressive, accepting anything that was given to her with great appreciation ... a quarter, a dollar. It didn't matter; she always smiled and said thank you. She did a very good job bagging too.

Ms. Sarah noticed that Celeste seemed to be there out of necessity, not to get some pocket change for snacks at the movies but to earn some money to buy some food, to survive. Ms. Sarah saw that Celeste wore the same clothes for sometimes two or three days at a time and that her hair was never done like a little girl's should be. She didn't know what or how, but she felt like Celeste was troubled, and she wanted to reach out to her without scaring her off or embarrassing her.

As it turned out, Celeste gravitated to Ms. Sarah easily and didn't shy away from her at all. Celeste needed someone to talk to, to be with, to share with, someone to comfort her, where she felt safe and secure, where she could cry.

Where she could scream.

For all her apparent strength in dealing with her family-affairs, school (she loved school and knew that getting a good education was her only ticket), and surviving on the street now and again, Celeste was lonely and afraid.

She was afraid for her mom and sister, afraid for her future, not sure what tomorrow would bring. When Celeste would wander back home after being away, her father would beat her. At first, it was more of the same old fear and pain. But after a while, she grew numb to the ordeal. She didn't even cry. She would just glare at her father with a deep hatred.

If looks could kill …

Her mom sensed this in Celeste and knew that her child had something inside her that was not going to let this devil defeat her, and she thanked G-d for it. Celeste would come home for meals, an occasional change of clothes, and to check on her mom and Sheila. She became their strength. When their father was away and Celeste was home, she consoled her sister and told her it would be all right soon and not to give up on herself or on their mom.

No matter how hard she tried, Celeste couldn't get either of them to fight back. She couldn't find a way to transfer her strength to them. Her father, after he realized that it had no effect on her at all, stopped beating her. He wouldn't even acknowledge her existence. But when she was home, he seemed to be extra cruel to her mom and sister. Celeste would later learn in her undergraduate studies at Penn that her father was afraid of her. He knew her strength and didn't want Celeste to inspire her mom and Sheila. So, he did what he could to keep them under foot, which was to be meaner, more brutal, especially in front of Celeste.

Celeste realized this, and as a little girl, she was powerless to stop him. She found herself staying away for longer and longer periods of time to avoid the painful reality of her helplessness and the anguish of the suffering of her mom and Sheila.

Ms. Sarah was her angel. She provided a place to go, a real roof over her head, food, money, companionship, a place to study ... a refuge and temporary peace. Celeste became the daughter that Ms. Sarah never had. She had two sons who were grown and on their own with sons of their own, no girls. After a while, Celeste didn't go home at all. She just stayed with Ms. Sarah, whom she took care of until she died ten years later from complications due to her congestive heart failure and stroke, basically just old age. Ms. Sarah was eighty-six when she passed.

By then, Celeste had graduated valedictorian from Dr. Martin L. King High School, and had graduated summa cum laude from Penn (no small feat from the elite of the Ivy League), and was in her second year of law school at Temple.

As soon as she was able to without parental consent (her father wouldn't sign), Sheila joined the army. She was killed in Iraq on her first tour of duty when her convoy was hit by a rocket.

While staying and basically growing up with Ms. Sarah, Celeste spoke to her mother on the phone whenever she could. Her father eventually developed cancer of the liver and died while hospitalized. He was cremated—no ceremony, no mourners. Celeste still felt a void in her gut stemming from her helplessness as a child, her inability to save her mom and Sheila.

Poor Sheila ...

She had joined the service only to escape, to wake up from the nightmare. Celeste knew that her dream was to become an engineer. Sheila was always good with stuff around the house; she could fix anything and was simply a wiz on the computer. Her mother would eventually develop Alzheimer's and have to be placed in a nursing home.

Celeste went to see her every night after work and always stayed for hours, sometimes overnight. She would just sit there and hold her hand, responding kindly to anything she said (whether it made sense or not), and when she fell asleep, Celeste would just sit there and cry.

Putting a plan together and working it to perfection, to put Romero away for a long time, came off without a hitch.

Shoulda picked some other haunt you monster

Impeccable police work, following all the rules, *no nightly beat down from the boys,* coupled with her brilliant courtroom savvy got her a conviction on all counts. In Angela's case, Celeste didn't go for battery in any flavor; she went for attempted murder and got it, hands down. The jury deliberated for only one hour.

After walking the beat and learning the streets, making arrests, getting a rep, Celeste was up for detective in no time, just three years on the force. A detective for two with the accolades accumulating on a regular basis, Celeste moved up the chain quickly in pursuit of her ultimate goal, assistant district attorney.

There, in that position, in that capacity, she felt that she could be the most effective in putting scum like Romero away. On the force, she saw all too often the fallacy of the system in letting the criminals get away because of poor or inept police work or simply bland prosecution. Celeste wanted to be instrumental in getting convictions. She learned how to figure people out and developed a knack for working the jury. She made them feel the victim's pain.

Her presence in the courtroom as a trial lawyer was like the virtuoso performance of a pianist at a final concert at the Walnut Street Theater—*simply masterful.* Presenting evidence in the most effective manner, at the right time. Getting witnesses to testify without fear. Getting deeply in touch with the women in the jury, finding ways to magnify the pain, abuse, rape, battery, and attempted murder that women suffered at the hands of men.

Celeste used her own personal experience to portray these hideous creatures for the evil they represented.

She found ways to connect with the men in the jury, to tap into the good that she knew was buried deep within their souls. It could have been their daughters. "Would you do this to your wife?" Her cross-examinations were something of legend. For anyone who took the stand in defense of these abominations, their testimony was soon destroyed and dismissed. Counsel for the defense knew that they were up against a mountain when they did battle with Celeste.

They had to put together cases that sought to lessen the punishment, rather than to seek an acquittal. Celeste didn't go after anyone she didn't feel she could put away, and to date, she had never lost a case.

Even if Celeste and the whole world knew that someone was guilty as sin, she wanted no part of it unless she felt with one hundred percent certainty that no defense could be mustered by any firm that would be able to pick the system apart to get their client off.

The DA let Celeste call her own shots because he knew two things for certain:

(1) Celeste wasn't after his job. She constantly reassured him that her maximum effectiveness in championing the cause for women besieged by the evil of men like her father (like her husband) was as an assistant DA, not the head honcho—too much politics.

(2) Celeste was good, very good.

She made him and the whole office look good. As much as Derrick was a political animal (or Mr. Evans, as Celeste always addressed him), the DA appreciated how everyone banned together whenever Celeste set her sights on a piece of vermin.

The rare times when Celeste refused to take a case, after explaining why, he knew she was right. The perpetrator would get off. There wasn't enough physical evidence. Witnesses wouldn't testify. Some police procedure was amiss, and the results thereof wouldn't be admissible in court. Whenever another assistant DA wanted to push on anyway, even after Celeste's warning, the prosecution would always have to plea-bargain down to a lesser charge and would sometimes lose altogether.

Celeste felt that if some creep got off easier than what was truly deserved, then it wasn't a victory at all. No, justice was not served. Sure, they would pay a visit to the *big house* for a while, but sooner than what was truly just, they would be back out on the street to prey on women again.

Celeste's approach was to make every effort, doing whatever was legally necessary, to put the scum away for as long as the law would allow. She knew that this could occur only if a conviction could be secured on all charges. The judges had the utmost respect for Celeste's work, because she was a student of the law and followed it to a tee.

They knew that in a trial where Celeste was the lead prosecutor, there would be no throwing out of evidence because of how it was obtained, no less than credible witnesses for the state, and no charges levied that could not be absolutely proven beyond a reasonable doubt. The judges had the responsibility to level the playing field.

They had to ensure to the best of their ability that the law of the land and the rights of every accused individual were upheld. They oversaw a forum in which it was the prosecution's duty to convince the court that the facts pointed to guilt.

The convictions that Celeste helped to secure happened simply because the truth was presented in a court of law. Celeste had an eloquent way of making everyone see it. The criminal justice system was her ally. Her courtroom demeanor was professional and passionate.

If you were in any way involved in any type of cruelty to women in the city of Philadelphia, if you were caught, if you were being prosecuted by Celeste W. DuPree, then you were going to get convicted, you were going to jail, and your sentence would more than likely be maxed out.

Celeste was able to dig deep into Romero's world. She got the support of the detectives' office who (out of respect for what Celeste stood for) stepped up their game and dug deep also.

Together, they were able to put together a case that revealed that Romero had beaten six other women over a two-year period, prior to Angela—not to mention he had a street hustle entrepreneurship that went back even further.

Romero was tried and convicted on all counts. Celeste knew that he was a predator. After seeing what he did to Angela, after hearing her story (Celeste somehow got her to relive it, detail by detail), she had no doubt that a trail of victims was out there somewhere.

The detectives found them, and Celeste convinced each and every one of the pretty lasses to come forward and tell their story, which were all different chapters in the same twisted saga of a wretched monster who had finally been caged, where he could hurt no one, no more. All told, Romero got over a hundred years in jail, to be served consecutively, basically... life in prison.

When word on the street spread that Romero had been clipped on this 'women abuse' beef, there were certain elements in the drug world who wanted to see Romero go down for a long time. Some because they didn't want to be connected to this kind of sickness; it wasn't cool, it wasn't honorable. They didn't like the fact that Romero could get away with something like this right under their noses.

Others because with Romero gone, his clients would need other suppliers—them. So, valid incriminating evidence started popping up all over the place, strengthening Celeste's case against him more and more.

Celeste sucked it all up, took in all in. If it could be validated and if it held up, she used it. Romero was fingered in a lineup as the shooter in an unsolved case a year ago, where some crew robbed him. At that time, the *big boys* squashed it and made them return the drugs and the dough.

He was their *cash cow,* so if you stole from him, you were stealing from them. The young thugs were *reprimanded* and told to leave Romero alone. But even after escaping with his life and getting his stash back, Romero went after them anyway, one by one. There were three of them. He beat two of them pretty badly (his forte) and used the last one's own gun and shot him in the back, paralyzing him from the waist down for life.

The drug and shooting convictions were a plus in putting Romero away for more time so that he wouldn't be available to prey on women. This is what Celeste was really about. Her relentless pursuit of men like Romero, who put their hands on women, sexually or otherwise, was fueled by her father's hell in the past ... and by her husband, Milton's, hell in the present.

Poor Celeste ...

How in the world did this happen? She woke up every day, looked in the mirror, and couldn't believe that the woman staring back at her was a victim of abuse. It couldn't be. This could never happen to the champion of battered women in this great municipality, to the one and only Assistant DA Celeste! No one would have ever believed it. In the blink of an eye, she could have the bastard behind bars where he belonged and where he would rot forever. She knew everything there was to know, everything there was to do. She had all the right connections to all the right people.

It was a no-brainer; one phone call, and it would be all over for Milton. Case opened, case closed. No drama, *tagged and bagged.* She wasn't afraid of Milton, not in the least bit. There was no fear. The first time he hit her (slapped her hard at dinner, at home one night, after an argument centered around his refusal to accompany her to some awards event in her honor ... again), she kicked him squarely in the balls, ran and got her .45 automatic, and was about to blow his freakin head off. Then Stacey walked into the room, their nine-year-old daughter.

She immediately put the gun away. Milton quickly grabbed Stacey and began to play with her. Celeste left the room, ran outside, got into her Benz, and drove off. She didn't know where she was going or what she was going to do. Her entire world had just come crashing down on her, and she was in shock. She couldn't believe that Milton had just slapped her.

Was he crazy? Did he truly understand what that meant? Did he stop to think of what she could do to him? Did he fully understand the severity of that action? She didn't think so; he couldn't have. Truth be told, in a straight-up fight, Celeste would have given Milton a run for his money, though she probably wouldn't have won. Medium build, about five foot seven and a half, Celeste was not a small woman, but Milton was the powerful, muscular type who had gender, height, weight, and more martial arts training on his side.

Celeste's police force training had long since withered away to weekend work outs at the spa. Milton damn near had his brown belt. Celeste was fiery and unafraid, but all in all, she was a woman. After she collected her thoughts, her calculating mind finally began to accept the reality she had been trying to ignore for years. It had finally caught up to her and hit her hard, *literally*. It was like she needed that slap to wake her up out of her daze. For years, she had seen the signs but chose to ignore them.

She dismissed them as shadows and innuendos that followed her into her adult life, memories from her childhood, and borrowed nightmares from the lives of the victims she avenged all the time.

Not her Milton, not her sweet, sweet Milton ...

He never would ...
He never could ...
He just did.

Even after the experience with her father, the personal tragedy that was her mother's and her dear sister Sheila's to bear, Celeste didn't grow up hating men. Ms. Sarah wouldn't allow it. She convinced Celeste that men were generally good and that sometimes circumstances beyond their control caused them to do things, bad things to the women they loved or cared for.

Ms. Sarah didn't actually believe that crap. She knew, just as clearly as Celeste found out later in life, that the Romero's of the world were personifications of a disease, a virus in the male gender of the human species that when identified (just like Sheila told her about the Trojan Horse computer virus) had to be isolated and quarantined.

Termination was unacceptable under the current laws of society and of G-d, and there were those who believed that these sick sons of bitches could even be *rehabilitated*. Ms. Sarah just wanted to spare Celeste from a miserable life of hate. She wanted her to have a normal life with a good man—you know, raise a family, live happily ever after, and all that.

Ms. Sarah's sons, James and Terrance, were wonderful examples of what men were supposed to be about—great sons, loving husbands, and wonderful fathers. In her personal development of identifying with the XY chromosome bearers, going from her father to Ms. Sarah's sons was almost surreal.

How could monsters like her father exist in the same universe with angels like James and Terrance? But after being removed from the midst of the sheer horror that was her father, coaxed and coached by Ms. Sarah, and intrigued with and truly loved by James and Terrance, Celeste became convinced that all men weren't evil, only some of them.

This allowed the natural desire to have a good man in her life grow and develop normally. Her father, the pimps and Johns on the street, all the *wannabe* boyfriends who only wanted to get into her panties (no one even came close)—all of these fools were soon dismissed from her psyche. They were reduced in importance and buried deep in the recesses of her mind. This opened the door for normality and allowed for Milton to happen. Sweet, sweet Milton. Even now as she sat in her car, no longer in shock, she knew with crystal clear clarity what had happened.

She began to reflect on her life with Milton, her teenage sweetheart from her junior year in high school, her only real lover, whom she eventually married and had Stacey with—their beautiful daughter, their precious little princess. Even now, she knew that Milton wasn't evil.

Celeste loved her husband with all her heart and soul. She would have never believed in a million years that what Ms. Sarah had explained to her about her father would apply to Milton.

Ms. Sarah (who had been absolutely right):

> Sometimes, honey, men go through things that cause them to change. It's hard being black in this world, especially for a man, honey. They don't mean to hit women. Sometimes honey, they get so full of anger and frustration, they wanna just lash out at the world, but they can't. It's got to come out, honey. So, they hit they wife or beat up on da kids. They don't mean to hurt them, but they do. You got to understand, honey. Don't carry all that hate and anger inside you, baby; it ain't gone do you no good. You got to let it go and trust in the Lord. He know what He's doin', and He gone make it all right. Just you wait and see. Look at James. Look at Terrance. I love dem boys. I give 'em plenty of lovin'. Look how they turned out. Your father didn't get much lovin', baby, and the world was hard on him. I'm not saying to forgive him, honey. I wouldn't ask you to do that. That's between him and the Lord. You just don't let it eat you up, baby. You gone find you a good man one day, baby. When you do, and you'll know it, give him all your love, honey. Make him feel special. I know you like I know my boys. You got a lot of love to give. You a sweet girl, baby. A sweet girl and strong. It's gone be all right. You gone be just fine. Now come on over here and give little ole Ms. Sarah a big ole hug, but don't squeeze me too tight now. My ole bones might break.

Milton was the reality that Celeste came to accept as the norm for men, just like James and Terrance. A senior quarterback for the King Cougars varsity football squad when she was a junior, he was sweet, not an arrogant, stuck-up prick like most jocks. She and Milton hit it off right away. Celeste was assigned to him via the school's peer tutoring program, an effort that promoted interdependence in the student body. Struggling students could get assistance from other students who were doing well. In theory, they could relate to one another better.

Milton needed help with English, and Celeste needed to come out of her shell. Milton was a people person and very popular, but he didn't hit the books hard. Celeste took him on as her special project. She went well beyond the parameters of the program and found herself entrenched in making sure that Milton *made it*. He scored low on the PSATs, and they knew that in order for him to play pro ball, his dream, he had to first get accepted into college.

This meant that he had to pass all his senior classes, finish with a GPA of at least 2.0, and do fairly decently on his SATs. Milton wasn't stupid or slow. If he applied himself in the classroom half as much as he did on the field, he would've been an honor student (well, at least above average).

But as it was, he was a great quarterback, and everyone kept telling him that he was going to make it big in college and eventually in the pros. They just forgot to mention the other part ... you know ... the part about getting an education in case the sports thing didn't work out. The part about how ball players should be student athletes and not just walking balls of testosterone who used their brains only to memorize playbooks.

Milton was convinced that he needed only to stay healthy, and then he could just skate by in life on his athletic ability. Charismatic, good-looking, and as far as most people saw in Milton ... a meal ticket.

Milton didn't mind this; he understood how the game worked (the professional sports game, that is), and he was willing to do whatever it took. He just wanted to play ball. He knew that if given the chance, he would shine. The money would come, and the fame would come. He didn't really care about the other fringe benefit of being a sports star; the women; he was a one-woman man. All he needed was Celeste.

They were inseparable, and she had his back all the way. She helped him study, and she was his PR person, his friend, his confidant, and his lover. No one could believe it when he turned down offers from all the top football schools—Penn State, Florida, Ohio State, Grambling, and many others—to stay in Philly and play for the Owls? Temple's football program sucked!

He explained that he wanted to go somewhere where he could make a difference. He wanted to stay local so that he could put Philly on the map. He was steadfast and adamant. Temple was ecstatic. They couldn't believe it. Although Dr. Martin Luther King High didn't win the public league championship (they never did) with Milton at the helm, they were finally able to beat their archrival, Germantown High, on Thanksgiving of his senior year, for the first time in seven years.

Milton's performance in that game had everybody talking; all the scouts were scheming. Everybody wanted him. Milton had already broken all of King's QB records—touchdowns, yards passing, yards rushing, and so on. But on that day, he was nothing short of masterful.

The Bears had a powerful offense and were sure to rack up the points on the Cougars' mediocre defense, and they did. But Milton kept them in the game, scrambling, finding open receivers. He was more than just a prolific passer; he was a born leader. He inspired his teammates and made them believe that they could win.

They just had to keep playing, keep fighting. His offensive line broke down that day and allowed six sacks. He was hurried, chased, and took hard hits at the last second to give his receivers time to get open. Every time, he would get up and shake it off like nothing happened. Hurting, sore, worn out, the boys didn't see that; they saw grit and determination.

With a record of 7–4, the Bears were a much better football team. The Cougars were 3–8. But on that day, Milton had the troops rallied. That day, they went on to beat the Bears with a last-minute scoring drive.

Announcer 1:

> Fourth and goal to go at the three yard line, the Cougars down 24–30, with seven seconds left on the clock. Tom, it doesn't get any better than this.

Announcer 2:

> You're right, Bill. This has been a nail-biter all the way. If you're a Cougar fan, you've got to love this guy Milton, win or lose. Whenever it looked like the Bears were gonna run away with it, like in the last seven Thanksgiving holiday classics between these two teams, Milton would somehow find a way to keep it close ...

Cut to the chase.

Milton ran it in for the score, the extra point was good, the Cougars won, and Milton was a hero ... once again. Celeste fell more in love. Milton stood tall and proud—in her face, in her life, and in her bed—as the true realization of her childhood dream, a good and decent man.

She never told him about her past; it didn't come out until she became assistant DA. Those who opposed her appointment tried to portray her as *damaged goods*. They argued that her pent-up rage and suppressed anger would manifest as a personal vendetta against men and would send some innocent guys to jail.

Milton was right there to support her, like she had always been there for him. The *picture-perfect* family scenario played in both of their favors.

His decision to stay in Philly, to go to Temple and play for the Owls, was a no-brainer. It was simple. Milton and Celeste had found each other. They fed off each other's respective strengths and needed each other. They were madly in love, and nothing was going to separate them.

He was the man. He was in control. It was his life, his career, and he made it clear to everyone: if he didn't play college ball locally, then he wouldn't play at all. He also knew that when going pro, he wouldn't have that kind of power. In the draft, you went with whomever selected you.

So, Penn was not an option. Milton was not Quaker material. St. Joe's, Drexel, La Salle, even Rutgers or some other close New Jersey school. If the school had a football team and was within a five-mile radius, and if the school wanted him, the option was open; otherwise, no dice.

So, Temple it was. Celeste finished number one at King the following year, valedictorian and all. Milton even helped her with her graduation address; she was so nervous. She, however, *did* get accepted to Penn on a full academic scholarship. They decided to wait until she finished undergraduate school before they got married.

Milton was doing well at Temple (although the Owls still sucked) and was in line to be drafted in the first round. They both knew that their chances of Milton securing a spot on the Eagles was slim. The year that Milton entered the draft, the Birds hosted the NFC championship game (lost to Seattle, who went on to lose the Super Bowl to the San Diego Chargers), so their draft spot was way down.

Milton didn't hesitate to let everyone know where he wanted to play his pro ball. His *Philly fever* (as it was dubbed by the media) was just a mask. He wanted to be as close to Celeste as possible. It was exactly as Ms. Sarah had told her.

Celeste was the scholar, with a bachelor's degree (major in criminal psychology, minor in political science), an attorney at law, a police officer, a detective, and an assistant DA with a perfect conviction record for men who were truly guilty of multiple crimes that included some type of not-so-friendly interactions with a female. She studied, she knew, she could relate, she understood ... but Ms. Sarah had explained it in the simplest of terms ...

Celeste (reflecting on Ms. Sarah's wisdom*):*

> *"Sometimes honey, men go through things that cause them to change honey, its hard being Black in this world. Especially for a man honey. They don't mean to hit women. Sometimes honey, they get full of anger and frustration, they wanna lash out at the world, but they can't. It's got to come out honey. So they hit they wife or beat up on da kids."*

Milton got injured his second time playing in a pro uniform. Drafted by the New York Giants (what a blessing to be so close to home, to his beloved Celeste), he rode the bench for a season as the number two guy, until fate called him in on the last play of a drive (just like in high school). The starting quarterback was blindsided and rode a stretcher to the locker room with what would be diagnosed as a mild concussion.

Five yards from the goal line in the final game of the regular season, against the Eagles (of all teams), to decide who would get the last playoff spot, the play was designed as a pitch and sweep to the right, with the running back trying to cut the corner pylon for the score. Without telling anyone, Milton saw something as he lined up the offense for the play of the game. It was only second and goal to go, but there was time enough for only one play. Down by four, they needed a touchdown to win.

The defensive captain studied the Giants' lineup and was signaling sweep. Milton knew that if he ran the designed play, they would be stopped short; he could feel it. Instead, he faked the pitch and sweep, delaying the toss just long enough to draw the guards and safeties to the seeming battle for inches about to ensue. He kept the ball, rolled left, and skated untouched into the left corner of the end zone for the score and the win. The Meadowlands erupted. Everyone was stunned—the Eagles, the fans, and especially the Giants players and coaches.

So, once again, a last-minute decision resulted in an unassuming victory, and once again, Milton was a hero. Celeste fell more in love. (Just how deep was her love for this man? How far could it go? It was about to be tested.) At the press conference, Milton explained that the element of surprise was crucial; if the play had any chance of working, everybody, even his protection, had to pull right. He had to wait until everyone's momentum was such that no one could adjust in time to stop him from scoring the touchdown.

So be it. Celebration ... a star is born and all that. Against the Bears in the wildcard game, on their first play from scrimmage, after Chicago scored a touchdown on their opening drive, Milton was blindsided when his left tackle slipped.

No concussion but a stretcher and a broken passing arm—out for the playoffs. The Giants were deemed the Cinderella team to beat, winning seven of their last eight after starting 0–2. As it turned out, Chicago won 35–7. The Giants' third-string quarterback threw three interceptions, and two of them were returned for touchdowns. The Bears ran the table and went on to win the Super Bowl that year.

What a shame, what a blow. Milton never got to throw one pass in the NFL. After his injury and two surgeries, the arm never healed right, and Milton's career, his lifelong dream, which had been so close to becoming a reality, was shattered. So was Milton. So was his spirit. Celeste was there for him, of course, like she always was—comforting, nurturing, consoling, loving.

She, on the other hand, was moving fast toward her dream. Now, in her second year of law school at Temple, Milton's alma mater, Celeste was focused, determined, and doing well. This unfortunate incident not only changed the path they were on; it also brought about some major changes in them.

Milton withdrew from the world; usually outgoing, bubbly with a charming personality, a true people person, he became somewhat of a recluse. He didn't want to be around people anymore. He just wanted to be up under Celeste. He had a clause in his contract that gave him a nice *set of change* if he should ever suffer a career-ending injury.

The doctors declared it as such, not out of pity but because it was true. Milton could still throw, but his depth, accuracy, and timing were all off. He was no longer qualified to play quarterback in the NFL. With the money, he and Celeste were set for a while. He would support her through law school, she would join a firm, and he would find work doing something, anything.

It was fortunate (mainly because of Celeste) that they didn't jump into some lavish lifestyle once he became a pro. They stayed within their means and lived well within their income—his. Celeste became more and more outgoing, aggressive, and confident in her dealings with people.

She was far from abrasive but very convincing and generated an aura of truthful seriousness. She had the *gift of gab,* which she cultivated. She developed into an eloquent speaker. Down to Earth but fiery and passionate, Celeste convinced Milton that they should get married right away.

Initially, they had planned to get hitched after she finished Penn, and then it was delayed until after Temple. Celeste wanted their love to grow even stronger. It was her way of convincing him that she wasn't going anywhere, that she was in it for the long haul. She loved, supported, and truly adored her Milton. His pain was her pain. She vowed that their world—hers, his, and the baby she was planning to have—would be perfect ... beautiful ... special.

What about now, Celeste? What about now?

The Voice again. Celeste didn't try to figure out where this Voice was coming from; it was somewhat soothing and vaguely familiar. Celeste and Milton had a lot of history. They had endured and shared a lot together, as one.

The good times:

- Milton's high school and college football days
- Celeste in college, in law school, passing the bar
- Their wonderful marriage (honeymoon in Spain)
- The birth of Stacey, their beautiful little girl
- His full-time parenting of Stacey as Celeste rose to become a powerful assistant DA

And the bad:

- The death of his father, his rock, his idol, who succumbed to prostate cancer
- Celeste on the police force (which he begged her not to join; he wanted her to become a lawyer after passing the bar, afraid that some thug's bullet would end their solace)
- Milton's pro football tragedy
- His drinking binge
- His accident on the job as a FedEx driver (no one got hurt, so the cops and the company didn't broadcast that he was DUI; his wife being a well-respected officer caught him a break, not his football notoriety, but they fired his dumb ass anyway)

None of the bad times excused the bastard for putting his hands on her. In the deep recesses of her mind, Celeste always knew (or so she thought) what she would do if Milton even acted like he was about to hit her. It would be the end of the story. Case closed. He would burn.

But he just did, and here she was rationalizing, trying to *understand,* wanting to forgive him, dismiss the whole thing. After all, it was a one-time thing; it would never happen again.

Bullshit ...

If anyone knew, Celeste knew that once it started, it was very hard for a man to stop, and the victims just found themselves deeper and deeper in a pit of unwarranted shame, embarrassment, and fear that would get harder and harder to climb out of. What transpired next could only be classified as *truly amazing.*

Celeste sat in her car and worked out a clear plan of action. What she figured out as the *way to deal* with this was as if she was outside her body, listening to another woman *explain* how she handled the situation ... how she had *no choice.*

This was not the same woman who appeared at countless group meetings for battered women, where she was always the honored guest speaker, telling the truth, setting the record straight, convincing the inconvincible, the scared and desperate women of the right thing to do, showing them the path and then guiding them along the way.

At any other time, coming from any other woman, her thoughts would have been easily dismissed as wrong—not the right thing to do, under any circumstances. But in this case, her case, it was the *only* thing to do. Celeste truly believed it, even though it was unthinkable.

Celeste decided to endure and appease ... once again.

The first time, it was for her mother and her sister; now, it would be for herself and her little girl. She was not ready for her whole world to go topsy-turvy, turned inside out, not wanting to flip the script, not wanting the world to know that the champion of battered and abused woman everywhere was herself —abused.

She wasn't afraid of Milton, not in the least bit. She wasn't embarrassed or ashamed and didn't feel responsible in any way. She understood that this onset of evil was purely Milton's fallacy, a result of his inability to cope, to deal. His weakness in seeking a scapegoat (her) was no different than the rest of his kind, those pathetic excuses for men. They all shared the same illness.

Every ounce of her being knew that Stacey was safe. And as time would tell, she was right. Milton would never directly hurt Stacey, mentally, physically, or otherwise. He loved his daughter, and she loved him back in a special way that was truly beautiful.

Stacey's world had to remain intact—perfect in every way, with loving parents, a loving home, everything Celeste never had. How could she take that away from her? She couldn't. (Milton didn't. His abuse directed at Celeste was never in front of Stacey; he was very careful to maintain the illusion.)

In time, Celeste was convinced that she would find a way to explain to Stacey that Daddy wasn't bad. She was even prepared to convince her that it was all Mommy's fault, if it came to that. If Milton continued (history had proven that men either have the capacity to abuse or don't, it was just that simple), she would do whatever it took to keep the soon-to-be illusion of a *wonderful family* going—for herself and for her little girl.

Was this the dilemma that her mother had faced? Maybe so. Maybe now she understood how she felt. Her mother may have dealt with it in a slightly different way, but she was sure that at some point in her life, her mother had to rationalize their sorrow too. What a shame. For Milton, she had a plan. She would give him the power and control that life had robbed him of (what a crock) that he somehow regained in hitting and dominating her (so he would think).

As a trial attorney, Celeste had developed pretty good acting skills, which she sometimes implored to woo a jury or a judge, however subtlety, and she was quite convincing. Now, she would play the *somewhat frightened, somewhat confused* role until she was ready, until Stacey was ready for her to set things in order. In reality, she would be in control, not him. Could she do this? Could she really allow him to abuse her?

In her mind, it was the only choice. She had to, so she did.

Celeste (speed-dialing Milton, waiting for him to pick up ... five rings):

> Answer the G-d damn phone, you-son of a bitch.

Milton (picking up):

> Hello?

Celeste:

> Where's Stacey?

Milton:

> Where the hell do you think she is? She's in her bed. Where the hell are you?

It had already begun. Milton had never talked to her that way, never cursed and never used that tone. He was probably just as shocked as she was that he had hit her. And now he had a choice—apologize, beg for forgiveness and hope and pray that she would accept his plea, get some help, and try to keep their marriage together ... or play the tough guy and follow this dark path to wherever it would lead them. He chose the latter. It didn't matter. Celeste already knew what she had to do. She had a plan.

Milton:

> Never mind. I don't care where you are.
> Bring your ass home ... right now.

Click.

Oh well, here you go girl. Good luck baby.

Celeste drove home. She pulled into the driveway and quietly went into the house, a moderate twin in the Mt. Airy section of Philly, considered by most to be the best neighborhood in Philly. Quiet, clean, and no drama. Milton was sitting at the kitchen table puffing on a Newport. (He had quit a year ago, with Celeste's help, then picked it up again, along with drinking, after it became apparent that he would never play pro ball again).

Celeste (in the sweetest, softest, sexiest Voice she could muster):

Hi.

Milton:

> Who'd you call? Who'd you talk to? When are they coming to get me? I might as well slap you around some more. I mean since I'm going down anyway. Earn my time in the can.

Celeste:

> No one's coming to get you. I didn't tell anyone. Milton, I didn't make the call. Whatever this is, whatever you're going through, whatever just happened, we can work it out together, like we always do. Just you and I, baby. I've never given up on you before, and I'm not going to now.

Saying those words made Celeste literally sick to her stomach. She couldn't believe they actually came out of her mouth. It was like she was rehearsing lines for a part in a terrible, low-budget horror movie, *simply disgusting.*

Cut to the chase.

Initially, Milton was afraid he would suffer the same justice that all of Celeste's "clients" were privy to. But as time went on, as he continued in his newfound *bad-boy* role, he was convinced that she would spare him for the sake of the family. Deep down, somewhere in there, he had a vague idea of why but couldn't quite understand.

He wasn't, after all, the sharpest pencil in the box. It became apparent that Celeste was trying to *maintain*, so he helped her and only let loose on her verbally. The physical molestations got progressively worse in private, although never in front of anyone, never in front of Stacey.

His actions, his life became like a lie you've told yourself for so long, that you began to believe it yourself. He had started down this path, gotten on this train, and didn't know how or where to get off. *Is this really happening? Why does this feel so good? What am I doing? Why? How did I get here? Have I lost my mind? What the hell is wrong with me?* Milton would ponder these questions from time to time in an attempt to understand his sudden Dr. Jekyll-Mr. Hyde persona.

Celeste never did. That first time, now one year ago, when she drove off was the only time she *thought* about it. Celeste just *lived* it. She had enough to deal with. Milton's issues, his problems, his concerns, and his thoughts were just that—his.

She had to focus on continuing her campaign against Milton's secret brothers, protecting her family's illusion, protecting Stacey. But it was taking its toll. It was eating her alive internally. She suffered in private. It seemed that Milton and Stacey were getting closer and closer. Whenever school events came up, Milton was always there. Mommy had to work.

She would make it on occasion, but Daddy was always there. Stacey would understand, because Daddy would always explain how important it was for Mommy to help catch the *bad men*. It pained Celeste to be away from Stacey, from home so much, but she had to. Becoming a workaholic was a way for her to deal, just like in her childhood when she would escape to Ms. Sarah's house.

There were times when she would wake up and think of putting a bullet in Milton's head. She was losing the battle to keep the farce going. Her true self was surfacing. How much longer could she keep this crap up? Someone was going to get hurt for real. Milton's *abuse* amounted to things she was getting sick of accepting—the occasional slap, the condescending tones and insults, the rough sex on demand (it wasn't rape because she always gave in; he never forced her).

When, Celeste? When?

The voice came more and more frequently. Celeste knew that if she didn't listen to it and *plan* her way her way out of this nightmare, just liked she had *planned* her way into it, it was going to end one way or another, really soon. She couldn't fake this bullshit anymore. Milton's life was hanging by a thread, whether he knew it or not. Each day that she lived was another day when the plots to kill Milton and dispose of his body became more and more appealing. What about Stacey?

She loved her daughter dearly. What was she to do? How was she going to end this charade? The Voice always asked her when but never told her how. She needed help; she wanted suggestions that didn't result in Milton, her baby girl's daddy, in a body bag.

All of the scenarios, all of the solutions that played out in her mind, ended up in disaster ... usually with Milton dead, her in jail, career shattered, and Stacey in foster care. *(These days, he had completely turned, and she suffered straight beat downs. He sensed that she wasn't really afraid of him, which infuriated him even more. She stayed away at length sometimes, just to avoid Stacey, until she could explain her scars. One time she lied and told her that a defendant attacked her in court. Milton later laughed in her face at this and told her it was a damn good story and she shoulda been an actress.)*

Stacey in foster care?

Now *that* was totally unacceptable, out of the question—not going to happen.

So, what then? *Come on, smart girl. You dreamed up this perfect scenario that's allowing this shit to continue, so get yourself out of it. Follow your own advice, the advice you gave to hundreds of women. They believed you, and your suggestions worked. So why is it so hard to save yourself? Save Stacey? She's a big girl now ... ten. She'll understand; she has to. Tell her. Make her believe you. Make her understand like Ms. Sarah made you understand that sometimes good people do bad things.*

Now that would be a hard sell. To Stacey, her father was an angel sent from heaven. There was no way she would accept it. All she knew, her whole life, her whole world, was Mommy putting away bad men, unlike her daddy. Milton knew this was his *ace in the hole,* and if it ever came down to it, he would use it.

She had to come up with an out, a plan of deception to get Stacey away from Milton without suspicion, without cluing him in to her scheme … to take Stacey and split, run away for good, leaving it all behind. She knew one person, one man she could trust to help her, Captain Williams over at the Thirty-Fifth. He would understand. He would help her ... and he did. Weeks it took her, weeks to get up the nerve to talk to Captain Williams, but she finally did. She didn't know that Captain Williams, who she worked under for two years, cared for her deeply.

He wasn't in love with her, but Celeste had his heart. He knew of her past service as a fine officer and followed her development into a superb assistant DA. He watched her put away creep after creep, in spite of the racism and sexism that reared their ugly heads in the department and within the criminal justice system altogether.

She persevered and rose to the occasion. The city was a better place with Celeste doing what she did, being who she was, and he had her back all the way. Captain Williams could appreciate all of what she stood for.

So, when she called him at 9:20 p.m. one Saturday to meet her at the Broad Street Diner, he assumed she had the lead on another creep she needed help to corral. He was right, but he would have never guessed that it was her own husband, Milton.

He watched their fairy-tale marriage closely, looking for signs. Signs that never came. She was always honest with him and never indicated once that he had hit her ... because he never did. Through all his trials and tribulations, the sports thing, and the FedEx DUI accident, Celeste never once suggested that she and Stacey were at risk. Captain Williams believed she was handling her business, like always.

She told him everything. She cried, laughed, and was completely spent. He listened and felt sorry for her. He commended her for her courage and *acting* ability. Celeste told him that she had to fake it well, or he was sure to find out. Captain Williams knew her like a book and was disappointed in himself that he hadn't seen any signs. It was just the way Celeste had played it.

Now what? She needed help to execute her escape plan. Captain Williams knew she wasn't running away, per se, just trying her best to minimize the effect on Stacey when the truth came out. They worked it out to perfection. Next week, Celeste would tell Stacey that she had a big surprise for her (she loved surprises) and that she couldn't tell Daddy. When the time came, Celeste took Stacey shopping at the Court at King of Prussia (not the gallery; she couldn't run into any of Stacey's friends or Milton's pool cronies).

There, she told her that they would be going on a trip. Mommy was given some badly deserved vacation time, and she and the family were going to Disneyland. First, she and Celeste would go. Then Daddy would come later, after she and Mommy spent some time alone together. About a week.

Things went off without a hitch. The Saturday after school was out, in June, they went shopping. That night, they were flying first-class to California.

Captain Williams had arranged and wanted to pay for everything. Celeste would never have allowed that. On the plane, Stacey asked when she could talk to Daddy. Celeste said she would call when they landed. She coaxed her into watching *Spiderman,* to relax and enjoy herself. That same night when Milton got home, Captain Williams and two plainclothes officers were waiting for him in the kitchen.

Milton (alarmed and somewhat frightened):

> Where's Celeste? What happened?

Capt. Williams (to Milton, all up in his face):

> Celeste and your daughter are fine, you little creep. They're far away from here by now. You'll be lucky if you see either one of them ever again. Your little charade is over.

> Celeste told me everything, from the first slap a year ago until last week when you beat the living crap out of her. The only reason why she didn't put a bullet in your head up until now, is Stacey. But you knew that, right? Couldn't have your brains splattered all over your little girl's pretty little dress, now could we?

Capt. Williams (addressing the officers, still glaring at Milton):

> Read em his rights and get this asshole out of my sight.

Milton was arrested without incident and was taken to the Thirty-Fifth. Capt. Williams emailed Celeste, and this time, she was glad to hear the *you've got mail* jingle. It was the signal for the end of an era.

She read the message from Capt. Williams informing her that Milton was locked up and that they could work out the details on charging and prosecuting him later. Celeste went to the bathroom and cried. Heavy, heart-wrenching sobs that rocked her entire being, her very soul.

It was finally over, and she could now focus on starting a new life with Stacey, her precious little girl. It was all over, all right, but in a sense that Celeste wouldn't fully understand until months later.

Stewardess (banging on the bathroom door):

> Miss, Miss please come out.

Celeste opened the door after wiping her face.

Stewardess:

> Please return to your seat and fasten your seat belt. We're coming into some turbulence.

Celeste:

> Okay. Is everything all right?

Stewardess:

> Yes, ma'am, just standard procedure.

There weren't many people in first class on this flight, as was usual on a Saturday night. Most business travelers flew during the week.

Stacey:

> Mommy, what's happening?

Celeste:

> It's okay, baby. I'm right here. Just some rough air up ahead. Don't worry. It will be just like riding a roller coaster for a while. Then it will be okay.

There was an elderly couple, two younger men, an older gentleman, tall, seemed to be in his fifties, wore glasses ... and them. They were all calm and didn't seem to be nervous at all. This helped to settle Celeste; she fed off this to help settle Stacey.

As much as she could with the seat belts restraining them, Celeste hugged Stacey. The chops came. They lasted nonstop for well over three minutes, and then they came sporadically.

Celeste:

> Stacey, stop crying, honey. It's okay, baby.

It wasn't.

Suddenly, there was a loud boom, followed by a high-pitched whistling sound. The plane listed sharply to the right, and Stacey starting screaming.

Pilot to copilot:

> We just lost the starboard engine. We'll have to level her out. Call it in. I'll disengage the autopilot.

Copilot to tower:

> This is Flight 78 out of Philly International, calling tower. We have a situation here. Come in, tower. Do you copy? 78 out.

No answer, just static. Finally, after a long silence:

Crackle, crackle, hsssssssssssssssssss, crackle ...

Tower:

> This is flight control. Go ahead, 78. What's your status?

Copilot:

> This is copilot James Stevens. We have a blowout of our trijet starboard engine, autopilot disengaged. Capt. Johnson and I will attempt to level her out. Keep this channel open. We'll keep you posted. 78 out.

Tower:

> Roger that, 78. Good luck. Tower out.

The intercom system came on.

Stewardess:

> Please remain calm. Everything is under control. Please stay seated and strapped in. The captain will speak to you in just a moment.

Copilot to pilot:

> We're gonna have to descend to flatten. There's not enough power to pull her up.

Pilot to copilot:

Not only that, but we have to land; we can't take her the distance on two engines. I'll inform the passengers. Call tower. Get us a strip.

Copilot:

Roger.

Pilot (addressing the alarmed passengers over the intercom):

Attention, ladies and gentlemen. This is the captain speaking. We've just lost our right engine. It's okay; we have two more, both of which are working fine. We're gonna have to come down a bit to straighten her out. After that, we're gonna have to land and switch planes. Don't worry; this means that you'll all get an extra meal. Hold on, folks. Everything is going to be all right. We'll be safe on the ground in just a few moments. Please stay seated, strapped in, and just try to relax.

Copilot to tower:

78 to tower. Come in.

Tower:

Go ahead, 78.

Copilot:

> Still descending, attempting to flatten her out. We'll need you to clear a path for an emergency landing. Captain says that two engines won't cut it for the distance. 78 out.

Tower:

> Roger that, 78. The nearest hub is O'Hare. We'll get you a lane. Level her out. Then we'll guide you in. Tower out.

Cut to the chase.

They couldn't get her leveled out. The plane kept descending .. 30,000 feet .. 28,000 feet .. 25,000 feet. They were still listing heavily. The port engine begin to sputter, something popped and somewhere in coach a lady screamed as a crack appeared in her window. The oxygen masks popped down as the cabin began to lose pressure.

Stacey:

> Mommy! Mommy! I'm scared! I want Daddy!

Celeste didn't know what to do, what to say. She was totally unprepared for this. She had to struggle with Stacey to keep her mask on. After getting her to take in some oxygen, she put the mask on and breathed deeply. Stacey, then Celeste. The lady still screaming, the stewardess over the intercom, still consoling, the plane still listing, still descending ... Stacey still crying ...

Celeste to Stacey:

Breathe, baby. It's going to be all right.

Celeste breathing in deeply ... It wasn't oxygen; it was more like sodium pentothal. She began to get dizzy, and all she could think about was Stacey.

Celeste (praying):

Dear G-d, not like this, not like this. Please, please give me another chance. We have so much to make up for. I love her so much ... I owe her so much. Please, please ...

Celeste began to fade. The last vision she remembered was of a tall man with the glasses, standing over her, looking at her calmly, seeming to talk to her without moving his lips:

You're going to be all right, Celeste.

Capt. Williams was right, but he couldn't have known it. He told Celeste's husband, Milton, the night he arrested him that he would be lucky if he ever saw his wife or his precious daughter again.

He never did.

No one did.

The Boeing 727 lost its port engine twenty minutes after the starboard engine blew. A chunk of metal cracked a passenger's window, which eventually broke, the cabin pressure decreased, and the pilots couldn't level the plane out. It plunged from twenty-five thousand feet and crashed just outside of Chicago in a bellowing ball of fire that set a cornfield ablaze.

The evening news reported that all 122 passengers were killed, including the captain, co-captain, and two flight attendants. At the beginning of the flight, there were one hundred and twenty four people listed on the flight manifest. The remains of Celeste and the tall man with the glasses were never found.

Chapter 2 - Supplement

Captain Williams

He felt guilty. Somewhat responsible. After all, it was he who had arranged the flight. He set everything up. He couldn't believe it. When the flight went down, he was at home. He had someone at Philly International promise to keep him informed of the flight's progress.

He got the call at 11:01 p.m.

Capt. Williams:

> Hello.

Man at Philly International:

> George, its Neal. I'm so sorry, man. I'm so sorry. Turn on channel 6 …

Action News Report (somber and serious ended with):

> No one on the ground was killed.

Why do they always say that? Who the hell cares? Capt. Williams hung up the phone. He was stunned. What a waste. What a loss. He hung his head low and cried.

George Paul Williams lived alone in a modest dwelling in West Philly's Wynnefield section. A divorcee of three years, he was able to maintain his position as captain of the Thirty-Fifth district for over seven years.

He was at Celeste's graduation from the academy and was the only other soul on the planet who knew of her living nightmare with Milton. She was like a daughter to him. He had no children of his own. He was numb. He turned off the tube and sat in darkness for over half an hour. After a double shot (neat) of Grand Marnier, he got up and drove to the precinct. It normally took him about twenty minutes; this time, it took forty.

Officer on duty at the station:

> Hey, Captain. What's up?

Capt. Williams:

> Give me the keys, Jack. I'm letting the creep go (a long pause) ... His wife and little girl were killed in a plane crash.

Officer:

> Celeste? Celeste DuPree? Oh my G-d, what happened?

Capt. Williams:

> Watch the news. I don't wanna talk about it. Wipe the record clean. We never picked him up. Got it?

Officer:

> Sure, Captain. No problem.

Capt. Williams went down to the holding area. Milton was in a cell with two other men. They had just finished their iced tea and cheese sandwiches for the night.

Capt. Williams:

Mr. DuPree, get up. Let's go.

Opening his cell, he motioned for Milton to get out. He didn't cuff him. He just led him upstairs to his office.

Capt. Williams:

Sit down.

Milton did. He didn't say a word. All night, he was trying to figure out what was going to happen to him. Capt. Williams didn't feel sorry for Milton. He felt the loss much more deeply for Celeste than he felt Milton ever could. But he knew how close Milton and Stacey were.

Celeste had told him of their special bond. It was this knowledge that compelled him to do what he was about to do. He felt no compassion for Milton. When it all came out, Capt. Williams didn't want the DuPree name to get tarnished. He wanted Celeste to be remembered for the heroine that she was. He didn't want Milton to get any press as the creep who got away with the crime of the century ... abusing Celeste. So, he put it to him hard and straight.

Capt. Williams:

Listen to me good, Mr. DuPree *(suppressing the urge to grab Milton by the throat and choke the living shit out of him).* Celeste and Stacey took a plane to California to get far away from you, from your abuse. Celeste wanted to start a new life for her and Stacey. We were gonna figure out how to make you pay. Oh yeah, you were gonna burn. She never got the chance. Not for Stacey ... and not for you. The plane crashed. Everyone was killed. So now you have to live with this. The fact that you drove her away, drove her to this. You put Celeste and your precious little girl on that plane. When it all comes out, when the dust clears, I want Celeste, Stacey, and you to come up smelling like roses. Don't you go getting self-righteous on me now. It's too late for that. Your precious little secret died with Celeste, died with Stacey. No one knows but you and me, and that's the way it's gonna stay. You're free to go. I'll be watching you though. And if you ever put your hands on another woman, then you'll see me again, but I won't be coming to arrest you. Get my drift?'

Milton nodded.

Capt. Williams:

Then you'll be able to ask for a pass, to go upstairs, and ask Celeste for forgiveness yourself before returning to your little hot seat downstairs. You dig?

Again, Milton nodded.

Capt. Williams grabbed a squad car and drove Milton home. They rode together in the front, in silence. Upon arriving at his Mt. Airy residence, Capt. Williams watched Milton go inside. Then he drove off. He saw him only once more, at the funeral. After that, Milton sold the house and moved to Detroit.

Capt. Williams resigned. The loss of Celeste was too much for him to bear. He couldn't understand why. He had suffered loss before—his parents, both siblings, his ex ... all dead. Partners, countless victims, friends, other family members. Why was this one so hard?

There was something so special about her. He was so right. Celeste was special, more than he or anyone else who knew her would ever realize.

Wake up, Celeste. Wake up.

Chapter 3

Justen

The Bloody Paradise

By the thousands they come, without any conviction
To the call of their nations, tormented mission
Some come by air, others by sea, yet they all have one will
They were given no choice, only brainwashed … to kill

Of bullets and bombs, machine guns and tanks
If I kill this poor man, I'll move up in the ranks
They are all just pawns in a political war game
To desert means to die; to fight … means the same

Sending letters to his wife, thinking only of his son
"Honey, I'll be home soon, as soon as this war is won"
Up on the front line, fire rains down from the skies
"I'm hit!" screams poor Joe. He takes shelter … and he dies

What's the meaning of all this? What's the matter at hand?
All this noise and confusion over a little piece of land?
Good men are dying. It's hell to the bitter end
When this mess is all over … it will all start again

Of protests and pickets and words of condemnation
It's all utter nonsense to the people of the nation
To the soldier it is real; those bullets are live
So, he lives from day to day and fights only … to survive

But the leaders are all blind; the anguish they cannot see
So, they press onward to their goal, which is sweet victory
"A surrender! We've won! Your land is now mine!"
But the real loser in this game … is all of mankind

1:32 p.m. News reporter:

It's a very tense scene here, and as I'm sure all other broadcasts are reporting, the situation has escalated to a near international crisis. Most certainly, it is a national one for the US and Saudi Arabian governments alike. If you're just joining us, you're watching live footage of the American embassy in Riyadh, Saudi Arabia, as it is under siege. As far as can be determined at this time, a hostile group of Islamic militants have somehow managed to overtake the embassy Saudi security forces and are now holding the vice president, six Secret Service agents, and two high-ranking military aides virtually hostage. The siege occurred just after the US entourage arrived at the embassy. The Saudi Arabian government agreed to host a peace conference, which was scheduled with the president of Iran and his top aides. To hopefully defuse what some political analysts have called the imminent *Third World War,* as it has been confirmed that Iran has acquired nuclear weapons, much to the dismay of the international community at large. The Iranian party has not arrived at this point, and it is almost certain that they won't. The only thing that weighs heavy on the hearts and minds of the American people now, is the safety of the vice president and his party. Our prayers go out to all of them and to their families, with hopes of a peaceful, speedy end to this most alarming situation.

Justen knew of war. This was in spite of the fact that he had never fired or wielded a weapon of any kind in his entire life, not even a BB gun or a knife. It was his diligent study of war, however, (its manifestations and mechanisms throughout the ages) that had ultimately brought him to this point, here and now, with the real threat of losing his life by virtue of some madman's bullet.

Justen knew of war. He studied war—the causes, the strategies, the losses, the victories, all of them. He wanted to learn, to try to understand the root reason men waged war against their fellow man, so he could be instrumental in putting an end to it, forever.

As he sat on the floor of the Grand Hall in the embassy amidst the foray of Secret Service agents, the vice president, and Saudi security forces, barricaded in this plush room, safe *howbeit for the moment* from the guerrillas who stormed the embassy only an hour ago, his mind began to drift backward through time.

From the available communications, it appeared that they were trapped. No way out … and hopefully no way for the guerrillas to get in. Their apparent plan was to gain entrance, capture the entire party, hold them hostage, then use them as a *bargaining chip* in their efforts to defuse the Saudi Arabian government's attempts, however feeble (as it now seems), to play a part in the eyes of the international community of maintaining some semblance of peace in the region.

Iran, a longtime opponent and vehement enemy of Israel; Iran, demanding that Israel surrender territories acquired through long, hard-fought campaigns of war with neighboring Islamic countries and militant groups; Iran, who targeted the growing Israeli settlements, Israel proper, supporters of Israel, and Israelis abroad with constant acts of terrorism; Iran, who challenges Israel's very right to exist—had long been suspected of trying to develop a nuclear program, despite constant denials.

A possibility ... no longer. But now, an even darker, confirmed reality. The US government, leader of the free world, Western culture, and civilization, and their allies had to move quickly in an attempt to escalate peace talks. They had to play the role of catalyst in getting Israel to realize how serious the situation was, how they must now change their strategy and their viewpoint on the *threat* of Iran.

No longer a nation of moderate military capacity, coupled with overwhelming numbers of soldiers and ordinary citizens, trained from birth to believe that death *by any means* was just for their enemies, that they should be ready to sacrifice their lives at a moment's notice in the defense of their belief (the destruction of Israel and anyone who aligned themselves with the infidels), taking the lives of as many innocent people as they could with them ... no, those were the good old days.

Those were threats one could live with and deal with when words became actions. Now, Iran had become a nuclear power, a different kind of threat. One that could no longer be dealt with in the same venue (can't just sit around waiting, hoping that the bombs don't fall). Iran was now a major player in the game and had to be treated as such.

The ability to end millions of human lives at the flick of a switch made a compelling case to listen to a nation's government's viewpoints and opinions (not necessarily those of its citizens), heard on the international stage.

The US government knew this, thus the attempt at the now failed summit. The agreement was to meet with Iranian officials in their region of the world, on their stage and on their terms. The agenda was to discuss how to open up a dialogue between Iran and Israel. Israel had already agreed to follow suit and would meet with Iran at a later time in a neutral place.

But first, the US had to *crack the ice* and get the ball rolling. In a show of good faith, Saudi Arabia had agreed to play host to this summit, one of the most important meetings of the modern era. Of all the nuclear nations that now existed—the US, the Soviet Union, France, Great Britain, even China—it was unilaterally accepted that the *new kid on the block*, Iran, was the most unstable.

It was also generally accepted by this group of superpowers that having this capability went hand in hand with the understanding that you could never use it. In this day and age, with mankind having the seeming ability to wipe out its own existence, the effort to prevent nuclear proliferation was first and foremost on the agendas of those who had reached its pinnacle.

But once acquired, the effort shifted to being assured that in the course of human conflict and war, nuclear weapons would never be deployed. Justen knew of war. He was very much in touch with mankind's hell-bent fascination (and curse) with the ability to end human lives, through conflict after senseless, meaningless conflict. Throughout the ages, before, during (*and unfortunately it would now seem*) after his existence as well.

He had an uncanny ability to identify, isolate, and clarify the essence and intent of an individual to want to kill. Justification notwithstanding, the desire and means to end lives remained. There was a time in his life when he believed that his calling was to profile serial killers, but he soon came to realize that governments and their war machines were a bigger threat to mankind, for they had the capacity to commit genocide.

This ability that he possessed was from early childhood. It began with his own family. As he sat on the palace floor, amidst the others who shared his plight, all equally frightened but most not wanting to show it, Justen found his thoughts reflecting on his father, William David Samuels Sr., and his brothers, William Jr and David.

His father, a proud military man who served in Vietnam and in operation Desert Storm, who always boasted of the *line*, generations of service to America dating all the way back to the Civil War (for the Confederacy of course) and probably beyond, as a family honor. A proud man who somehow managed to emerge from his numerous military campaigns with his body and mind intact, a decorated war veteran.

A hunter always, ever since Justen could remember. As a little boy, Justen never shared his father's deep-rooted desire to take the life of another living creature by wielding a gun. Geese, rabbit, dear, bear ... it didn't matter.

Justen never thought it to be brave or divine. How about with a knife? How about with your bare hands? Give the poor creature a fighting chance. Justen realized from early on that mankind's dominion over other living entities we share the planet with, was not as it was so conveniently taught in school, *his ability to reason*, but rather the ability to create *death and destruction*. His seeming never-ending quest to find more creative and ingenious ways to accomplish it on larger and grandiose scales ... the hunt, murder, multiple homicides, war, genocide.

Justen's mother knew about this distaste for violence and death in her youngest son. She always came to his defense whenever a hunting trip popped up.

Mrs. Samuels (addressing her husband):

> William, leave that boy alone. If he doesn't find pleasure in hunting and killing things, then so be it. It won't make him any less of a man, and besides, you have two other sons to corrupt. Let him be.

In the beginning when he was of age, he would tag along with his father and two older brothers, William Jr., the eldest by five years, and David, older by three. He loved them, and they loved him. They were a tight knit family. Everyone knew and accepted that Justen was the most intelligent in the family but with a quiet sense of resolve and calmness.

Always respectful, always pleasant. Always wanting to help, to be a part, to belong. It was Justen who understood and learned what his father tried to teach his brothers about the art of killing–how to quietly stalk your prey, get them in your sites, aim steadily, and then shoot to kill.

Justen would master the lesson but would never exercise its objective. It was very important for William Jr. and for David to get the hang of whatever their father wanted them to learn. How to be men, and to live up to the Samuels' legacy of great hunters, military men ... killers.

Justen knew this and helped them. He caught on quickly to not only what Sir William wanted his boys to master but to everything else as well. He understood that his father's pride and love of hunting was the glue that held his family together. He loved his family.

Sitting on this palace floor, waiting for a sniper's bullet, mortar, rocket, or a hand grenade to end his life made him wish he was young again and back home. His brothers loved him for helping them to succeed in receiving their father's approval. Justen also helped them with their schoolwork, and he was always coming up with new and creative ways to help them accomplish their chores.

Justen was a born leader. He could motivate and inspire people to achieve. His brothers developed to their full potential (William Jr. a police officer, David a soldier) primarily through his tutelage.

His parents observed Justen's development closely, they knew of his gift and watched it grow. After a while, he stopped going on hunting trips with *the men*. He would stay home with his mother. She loved his company. He was such a wonderful son. He helped her with her duties around the house, improving upon and perfecting common tasks centered on cooking and cleaning. They had conversations about everything there was in life.

It was this early preparation coupled with his natural intellect that fueled his achievements in school—straight As in every subject and always at the top of the class. Nerd? Geek? Know-it-all? The usual accolades and labels that accompanied child prodigies like Justen never applied to him. His friends, peers, teachers—everyone who came in contact with Justen grew to like him and eventually to love him. He had what people called an *old soul*.

He had a way about him that made people feel comfortable, secure, and safe. There was an aura about him, an unseen force that attracted people to him. All the kids wanted to play with Justen, and all the clubs and frats wanted him as a member. Intelligence is of course sexy, so he always had a barrage of *ladies come to court,* but he would never abuse this power. If he had political aspirations, he would have been a shoo-in for office, any office—city council, Congress, governor, even the presidency. Throughout his entire life to date, Justen never made one enemy.

He even believed that if he could somehow get a chance to confront his present assailants (without a weapon in his hand), he could make them see reason. He would make them understand that violence is not the only way to resolve conflict. He would make them realize that death and destruction ultimately seek to undermine what everyone wants anyway: peace and prosperity, life and love.

Even if it meant risking his own life, if given the chance, he would try. You see, that's who Justen was. That's what he was built for. For all his intellect and abilities, Justen believed wholeheartedly in what he accepted as his mission in life, to defuse, resolve, and end human conflict that ultimately resulted in the loss of human life. That is what he was designed for.

One day, when the men were out on some hunting trip (to secure another trophy for the den), during one of those heart-to-hearts with his mother, she asked him:

Mrs. Samuels:

> So, son, what do you want to be when you grow up?

Justen (at age nine or ten):

> Nothing special, Mom. It's what I want to do when I grow up.

Mrs. Samuels (she struggled sometimes, just to keep up with him):

> Okay, Justen, so what do you want to do? Do you want to be a doctor or a teacher?

Justen:

> Maybe; it all depends. I'm probably going to have to learn a lot of stuff so that I can mix with as many people as I can. I want people to like me so that they will listen to me.

Mrs. Samuels:

> People already like you, Justen. I'm sure that you'll always have many, many friends. You're such a doll. You're good at a lot of things, son, but don't you want to be really good at something special, so that you can be really famous and make lots of money, you know ... and be on TV? We would be so proud of you.

Justen:

All of that stuff is really cool and all, Mom, but what I want is different.

Mrs. Samuels (totally confused, no clue whatsoever):

Okay, baby, what is it that you want?

Justen:

I want to learn about people. I want to learn about how they think. I want to understand why they do things. I want to learn how to make people change their minds about doing things. If I can get enough people, the right people, to change, then they will help me to change everybody else. When enough people have changed, then soon everybody all over the world will just stop ... and nobody will ever do it again.

Mrs. Samuels (smiling nervously):

What, Justen? What do you want people to stop doing?

Justen:

Killing other people.

Mrs. Samuels's smile just froze on her face. For a moment, she was just suspended in time. A cold chill entered her spirit and crept over her soul. Any other mother would have just accepted this as an innocent expression of a young child with a good heart. But if anybody did, she knew Justen; she knew her son. Mrs. Samuels understood that many people had dreams and goals.

That even as children, they would latch onto what they wanted for themselves, for their lives, and they would methodically go about the business of attempting to fulfill their aspirations. She also understood that along the way, people would sometimes lose track, get sidetracked or even change tracks altogether, eventually settling into another venue, not necessarily in the original game plan or even in the same ballpark.

Everybody but Justen.

Somehow she knew; she could feel it, she could sense it. She had no doubt in her mind that her little boy, her precious son, was serious. She knew that, with every bone in his body, with his every breath, until his very last, Justen would try to make his vision, his dream, a reality. She knew that he would never give up. She worried for him, about him.

What kind of life would that be? People are so cruel. People are so mean. Mrs. Samuels feared that Justen's quest for world peace would only be transformed into a *trail of turmoil,* into a *destiny of doom and despair.* How could she save him? How could she stop him? She knew that she couldn't.

She feared that Justen's *mission of mercy* would one day lead him to *desperation and death*—his own. Even though she couldn't see his future or know what truly lay ahead for her dear son, for her precious boy, Mrs. Samuels feared the worst.

This was the worst. Many a tight spot and many a close call had Justen known, had Justen survived. But this was different; this was deadly. These men, these misguided, *poor souls,* these terrorists, now held the power of life and death in their hands ... his life.

How did it come to this? Where did he go wrong? Why didn't he see this coming? Justen was so sure that this would be the beginning of a new era. The end of the *old-days* of man's deadly and destructive *old-ways* of conflict resolution.

If Israel and Iran could make peace between themselves, then the world would soon follow; it had to follow. And Justen would be right there, right in the middle, *in the thick of things* as a major player.

All his life, he dreamed of this moment, of this opportunity to make a real difference in the world, to help stop the killing and the threat of bloodshed. Now all of a sudden, in the blink of an eye, here he was as a hostage. Just another victim who was about to be sacrificed for another pointless cause.

No matter how much these idiots believed that their cause was just, that their actions were justified, Justen knew, Justen understood this to be exactly what it was—just another feeble, pointless attempt at resolving a meaningless conflict, with more death and destruction. That's all. That's it. Nothing would be achieved. Nothing would be gained. Not on any meaningful scale, the only important scale, the global scale.

No matter how it turned out, no matter who *won*, the world would lose, because once again, lives would be lost. Precious human lives would be destroyed for a minor shift in power, a mediocre, miniscule victory of sorts. This would set schemes in motion for retaliation. Another plan would be conceived, approved, and set in motion for yet another scenario.

But as Justen understood it to be, the same scenario would emerge ... different players, different stage, same result. To date, Justen had studied all these failures, following them to their logical conclusions, be it a minor coup or a major invasion.

He seemed to be the only soul on the planet who understood that if these so-called *victories* could be achieved only by death and destruction, then everyone was doomed. The seemingly never-ending escalation of conflict after conflict, coupled with the unfortunate technological achievements of the mechanisms of war, which led to today's terrible stage of the age of nuclear weapons, spelled certain disaster for mankind. This couldn't be, not here, not now, not again. There had to be a better way.

There is, Justen. There is.

That Voice again. Somewhat soothing and vaguely familiar. A constant reminder of why he existed, what his purpose was, what he was on earth to do. It began early in his adult life whenever he was faced with an immediate crisis that sought to end in bloodshed, in death.

Whenever Justen was attempting to defuse a situation, when he knew that there had to be a better way, he would hear the Voice whisper in one ear, and then repeat in the other, that very phrase. Soon after, a solution would come to him, and Justen would find a way, to save the day, to save precious human lives.

But not today.

Justen was seasoned, he *was* the sharpest pencil in the box. He knew that the minds behind the actions of these men, these pawns, sought not to just disrupt the talks; oh no, they wanted to start a war.

They wanted nothing less than to seize control (which they already had), flaunt their false victory on the international stage, then turn it into a true international crisis and subsequent disaster, by killing everyone they could ... the vice president, the Secret Service agents, the Saudi security forces, the other military aide, and him.

Justen was not about to have it end like this. He was beginning to see the fruition of his lifelong labor take shape, and he wasn't about to have these bastards steal it away in an insane blaze of *non-glory*. You see, Justen knew. He was an inside man. The US military had adopted a new hostage situation policy that was in full effect ever since 9/11, code-named ASS-NET, short for *assess and neutralize*. These idiots had sealed not only their fates but those of the hostages as well.

The US elite forces were coming in—Navy SEALs, Green Beret, Army Rangers, it didn't matter, whoever was closest with a team ready that could be deployed immediately. Whether people realized it or not, as a US citizen traveling abroad, or as a US government official or political figure deployed on some diplomatic mission, they accepted two realities if they were taken hostage:

(1) The US government would send in a negotiating team. They would listen to the demands of the hostage takers, discuss requests, and make every attempt to assure them that their ultimate goal was the preservation of human life.

(2) At the same time, from the initial moment when news of the crisis hit the airwaves, military mobilization was already underway. Oh yeah, they were coming in with *guns-a-blazing*. Hostage rescue? If possible, then so be it, good show, tally-ho, and if not, oh well, too bad, so sad.

In any event, the thugs would perish, all of them. Then Intel would be dug up as to who was responsible, and they would perish too—wipe them out, all of them. It happened in Afghanistan a couple of years back and more recently in Pakistan. No one survived. Not the hostage takers, not the hostages.

Twenty-four people the former ...

(Eighteen bad, Taliban, six good.)

Seventeen people the latter ...

(Thirteen bad, Isis, four good.)

Justen was not about to join that group. Not today, not ever. In some circles, Justen was considered a military genius. For the last two administrations, he served as a top aide. There were those who opposed this appointment, mainly because he had never served one day in the armed forces. Then there were those who called the shots, who truly appreciated having him around.

Wherever he found himself, his reputation preceded him, which was that of a level-headed, cool, calm, and collected individual. He had an uncanny ability to assess a given situation and come up with a strategy to secure the best possible outcome. In cases that involved armed human conflict, his objective was always the same—a speedy resolution with the maximum preservation of human life.

The situation at present was no different, especially since one of those *human lives* was his own. That might have been the kicker, the catalyst, the spark that lit the flame. Never before had Justen been so in touch with his own mortality. This was not about humanity or some noble concept about saving mankind. This was personal; this was gut instinct; this was about survival.

A calm came over Justen, and just like a grandmaster chess champion in the midst of the *Middle Game* stage of the final game in a match to crown the victor in an international tournament, Justen did what Justen was born to do: he took command.

Justen:

> Okay, gentleman, listen up. First, is there anyone here who doesn't understand English? You don't have to speak it well, but it's very important that you comprehend. Gather around. Can everyone understand me?

A few of the Saudi security officers glanced at one another for a moment, then nodded in agreement and moved in closer to the circle that was forming around Mr. Samuels.

Justen:

> I'll make this brief, because we all know that we might not have that much time, so listen very carefully. My name is Justen Samuels. I am a top military aide to the executive office of the US government, which includes the president, the vice president, and the Joint Chiefs of Staff. Although we are in Saudi Arabia, this is a US embassy, and therefore we are under US jurisdiction. Mr. Vice President …

The vice president:

> Yes, Mr. Samuels?

Justen:

> You are the senior ranking official here, sir, are you not?

The vice president:

> That is correct, I am.

Justen:

> Then please, sir, introduce yourself as such to these gentlemen. Then transfer full and unrestricted command power to me, by authorization of Executive Code 1266.

The vice president:

Gentlemen, as the vice president of the United States of America, and as the senior ranking official here, and as this operation is under military jurisdiction, effective immediately, I hereby give Mr. Samuels full and unrestricted command power.

Justen:

Thank you, Mr. Vice President. Gentlemen, what just transpired is very simple. No one in this room is to take any action or make any move from this point forward unless it is by my direct order. Agents, if I feel that anyone here is a threat to my command, which would make them a threat to our collective survival, then I hereby authorize deadly force to neutralize that threat. Is that clear?

Secret Service agents *(in unison):*

Yes, sir, Mr. Samuels.

Justen:

My objective in taking charge of this situation is very clear. I want all of us to come out of this alive. So, whatever I ask of you, whether you understand my reasoning or not, please do not hesitate or question my judgment. Just respond to the best of your ability. Understood?

The hushed group together:

> Yes, sir, Mr. Samuels.

Two of the Secret Service agents and the vice president, unbeknownst to the rest of the crew, experienced a warm glow inside. They knew Justen. They had witnessed firsthand what he was capable of. They knew that if anyone could save their necks, Justen could. If they had to trust their lives to anyone, there was no better person on the face of the planet than Mr. Justen Samuels.

Justen:

> There is to be no communication whatsoever to anyone, unless it is in direct response to a question that I ask or to inform me of something you feel is vitally important. No more verbal acknowledgments of my orders. Just nod. Agreed?

(Affirmative nods from the group.).

Justen:

> Is there anyone here who has been shot or is otherwise injured?

(All negative head shakes.)

Justen:

> Agent Wilson, identify yourself by raising your hand.

(Agent Wilson responded.)

Justen:

> Agent Wilson is a medical doctor, a field surgeon and one of the best. If you become injured, if you're able, let Mr. Wilson know somehow, and he will come to your assistance. Everyone, empty your clips and spare ammo in the center here. I want all weapons accounted for. Do it now.

Inventory.

In addition to himself, the only other unarmed individuals were the vice president and the other military aide, Mr. Barns. There were six Secret Service agents. All of them had the standard issue of a .45 automatic with a backup snub-nose .38 Special. There was sporadic distribution of spent clips in the .45s, but the .38s were fully loaded.

All told, there were twelve spare clips for the .45s and six spare sets of rounds for the .38s. The Saudi security force numbered nine. Each soldier had an AK-47 semiautomatic assault rifle with sporadic discharge, but each man had the full backup of crisscross shoulder rounds. The Glock 9 mm they each had holstered were fully loaded, but not every man had backup clips.

Justen:

Okay, gentlemen, as much as possible I want even ammo disbursement. The vice president, Mr. Barns here *(tapping him on the shoulder),* and I will take a .38 and a spare round each. Lock and load, gentlemen. Saudi team, remove your sling belts for your rifles and carry them in your hands for easy access, or in case you have to pass them to someone else. Do it, gentlemen.

(Everyone responded and awaited the next order.)

Justen:

After I'm finished, break up into groups of two or three and await further instructions. Listen carefully, and we'll all survive this. My plan is as follows. In less than an hour, US elite troops are going to storm this embassy. Be assured, they're on their way, gentlemen. The militants on the other side of that door have already sealed their fate by attacking this party, and if we're not careful, ours also. When the cavalry arrives, they're coming in guns-a-blazing. They won't be asking any questions, nor will they be taking any prisoners. They won't allow us to be taken either. The only way we won't become casualties is to assist them in their efforts; we must become allies in their mission.

> I know their tactics, and I know their strategy. I helped to design their MO, and I know what they are going to do. Agents, disperse the red bandanas. Gentlemen, remove your covers and tie these around your foreheads. These will identify us as friendlies. They're fluorescent. Tear some clothing, a piece of your shirt or pants, long enough to cover your nose and mouth. They will use gas—our guys and probably the goons out there too. Keep it handy. Remove any sharp objects from your person. Remove any dentures, glasses. Remove your shoes, boots. Store your personal effects there. Tie them up. Do it.

(Everyone did as instructed.)

Justen (continuing):

> When I deploy you, position yourselves around the perimeter of this room. Space yourselves out; don't bunch up. Take cover. Use the desks, sofas, and chairs. Steer clear of that door and all windows. The bad guys are gonna blow the door and come through. Our guys will be coming through the windows. When they do, kill all lights; shoot them out. Then stay put and concentrate all your firepower on the door. There are no other ways in or out of this room. There are no hidden panels or secret passages.

> Check your targets, head and chest shots only. Conserve your ammo. We have no way of knowing just how many goons are out there. More of our guys will be bringing up the rear. But there's no telling how long it will take them to get through. If we can hold our own here, make a stand, then we'll catch those bozos in a crossfire, and all of this will be over real soon. I'd like to commend you all on making it this far. Don't give up now. Hang tough, true grit ... sure shit. If we work together, stay sharp and smart, we'll be home in time for dinner. Okay, gentlemen, take your positions and wait for my signal before engaging. I'll see you on the other side when the smoke clears. Mr. Vice President, Agent Wilson, you *(pointing to a Saudi security officer with an automatic rifle),* you're with me. Move, gentlemen.

Cut to the chase.

It went down just like Justen told them it would, approximately ten minutes after Justen gave his final orders. The boys waited for what seemed like an eternity—complete silence, no movement, no coughing, and no sneezing. It was the longest ten minutes of their lives.

Muffled noises were heard outside the locked, reinforced steel embassy door ... faint voices. Then came the deafening explosion as the door blew completely off its hinges. Smoke and teargas followed. The guerillas continued their assault, creeping into the room and shooting in all directions.

Justen (waiting until the goons were all the way in, screaming at the top of his Voice):

TAKE THE BASTARDS OUT!

The boys joined the fire fight, which lasted for over three minutes. The US commandos came crashing through the windows, as if on cue—north, west, and east, all at the same time. The crew was just about out of ammo, but they had managed to hold off the bad guys. They were still alive.

The Saudi security officer who was with Justen took out the lights, and the commandos, now able to identify the team via the bandannas, advanced past them and engaged the guerillas. The rear guard had arrived. They formed a solid wall of resistance and were driving the goons into the room. The troops were collapsing on the enemy who had nowhere to run, no way to escape; now they themselves, were trapped.

It was all over in a matter of minutes. There were no additional casualties for the good guys, other than the six Saudi security officers and the one Secret Service agent who perished during the initial siege. During the last moments of the battle, when the commandos were converging on the guerillas from all angles, Justen took two rounds as he shielded the vice president, one in the chest and one in the stomach.

After the dust settled and the commander of the elite forces signaled that all hostile forces had been neutralized, all dead, Agent Wilson began to work on Justen.

Agent Wilson:

> I need a med kit over here quickly. Mr. Samuels has been hit.

Commando leader:

> Mr. Vice President, we have a chopper standing by. Please come with me, sir.

The vice president (standing over Justen as Agent Wilson bandaged his wounds and was preparing to give him a sedative):

> Soldier, is the area secure? Has the enemy been subdued?

Commando leader:

> Yes, sir, Mr. Vice President, for the moment, but the longer we remain, the more at risk you'll be. My orders are to get you stateside, at all costs. We have to move, sir—now.

Justen (faintly):

> As the commanding official on the scene, Mr. Vice President, I'm ordering you on that chopper ... or I'll have you shot. Agent Wilson, if this gentleman is not out of here in one minute, carry out my orders. Understood?

Agent Wilson:

> Yes, sir, Mr. Samuels.

He took out his firearm (empty clip ... safety on) and laid it on the ground where Justen could see.

Commando leader:

> A medevac is on its way, sir. ETA six minutes.

The vice president (leaning over Justen, gripping his hand firmly):

> I'll expect you in the Oval Office at 0800 hours, two days from now, for a debriefing with the president. Mr. Samuels, don't be late.

Justen (nodding, almost out from the sedative):

> Did everybody make it? Are we safe? Where's the ...

The last thought didn't formulate completely as Justen faded out.

The vice president to Agent Wilson (with a feeble Voice and tears in his eyes):

> Is he going to be all right? Is he going to make it?

Agent Wilson:

> His wounds are pretty serious, sir. I've managed to stop the bleeding, but I can't tell how bad his internal injuries are at this point. I'll contact you immediately once we're on the medevac and I can better assess his condition. (Slight pause) We're going to do all that we can to save him, cause he sure saved our necks here. You just head on back to the States, sir, and get that Congressional Medal of Honor ready, Mr. Vice President.

The vice president:

> I know what you mean, son. I know exactly what you mean. Take care of him. See it through personally, all the way to his full recovery. (Turning to the Commando Leader) Let's go.

The vice president, Mr. Barns, the Secret Service agents, and the Saudi security officers were all escorted to an awaiting Black Hawk, which took off without incident. No one else in the party had been shot or otherwise injured—only Justen. Agent Wilson remained with Justen until the medevac arrived, exactly five minutes after the vice president's chopper left. Two paramedics carrying a stretcher came to where Justen and Agent Wilson were waiting.

Agent Wilson:

> The bullets are still inside, two rounds. Do you have x-ray equipment on board?

Paramedic 1:

> That's affirmative. Is he fully sedated?

Agent Wilson:

> No. He'll be awake momentarily. I gave him just enough to keep him out while we moved him. Although he didn't allude to it, I know he is in a great deal of pain. Let's get him outta here.

Justen was gently placed on the stretcher and taken to the chopper, which also took off without incident. On board, he was stabilized and given oxygen. The subsequent x-ray revealed one bullet, which had pierced his right lung (collapsing it) and was stuck in the back of his rib cage. The other was lodged in his stomach wall.

Instructions came in for the pilot to head due west for a US Navy ship in the Persian Gulf, anchored just off the coast of Kuwait. It was fully equipped and staffed to operate on Justen. It was also the most secure location in the region, which offered the best defense in case there were further outbreaks of hostilities. As the medevac approached the Gulf, Justen awoke.

He was still a little groggy, but amazingly, he was in no pain whatsoever. He could barely make out the silhouette of a tall man wearing glasses leaning over him. Justen's mind flashed back to the day he had first arrived at the embassy with the vice president and his party. He remembered his excitement as the prospect of peace in the region seemed within their grasp.

Justen (thinking to himself):

> *Israel and Iran agreeing to start peace talks? What a wonderful omen! What went wrong? What happened? Is this it? Have we failed? Have I failed?*

You'll get another chance, Justen.
You'll get another chance.

The Voice again. This time, Justen could clearly make out that it was coming from a tall man with glasses leaning over him ... without moving his lips or opening his mouth. Justen faded out again.

The medevac never made it to the navy ship. A surface-to-air rocket, fired from a guerilla ground unit, scored a direct hit on the chopper, which exploded into a million pieces and sank to the bottom of the gulf.

A recovery effort was never ordered.

Chapter 3—Supplement

In Memory

Never before in American history had one individual been awarded two Congressional Medals of Honor. Justen was the first, even though his second was given posthumously. The funeral was broadcast on all major channels, with full military honors. Justen was laid to rest (empty coffin) at Arlington National Cemetery in Washington, DC. At the interment, his widow, Mrs. Susan Samuels, was presented with two flags, one from the president of the United States of America, the other from the prime minister of the Kingdom of Saudi Arabia.

All government facilities, aircraft carriers, and warships were ordered to fly their flags at half-staff by land, half-mast by sea—a most appropriate tribute for a national hero. For nearly two and a half decades, Justen Samuels was an instrument of peace and a Voice of reason in the hierarchy of the US government. He always advocated for peaceful resolutions to armed human conflicts that could ultimately result in the massive loss of human life.

Speaking at Justen's funeral (which was held at the Cathedral of St. Matthews in Washington, DC) the vice president of the United States of America made it clear to everyone present that although Justen was a consummate man of peace, he was also a military genius.

In the absence of a nonviolent solution to a conflict, his vision and ingenuity to develop strategies that sought to minimize human casualties, by securing clear and decisive victories, was legendary.

The vice president:

> If we as men and women of the human race do not learn from his legacy, then our honoring him here on this day will be in vain. Justen Samuels was concerned not with securing military victories but with sustaining human existence by eliminating the need for military campaigns altogether. And I quote: "*The multitude of cultures and peoples that share this planet must find a way somehow to use our differences to unite us and to enrich our human experience. We must discover, design, and introduce strategies that break down the barriers that divide us, that foster death and ultimately our destruction.* "I have been changed by knowing Justen. By working with him, I have been infected with and have reaped the benefit of his pure and unadulterated compassion for human life. If enough of us are infected, if the legacy of Justen Samuels spreads throughout the leadership of the nations of this earth, then there will never again arise the need to grieve over the loss of life as we are here to do today ...

Why are we here? Why do we exist? No matter what anyone's beliefs are, no matter what your faith, no matter what flag you pledge your allegiance to, somewhere in your dogma, the ultimate concept of peaceful coexistence must be a high priority. We must all work together to achieve this. If not, then we are all doomed.

How true, Mr. Vice President. How true.

Justen Samuels knew this. He tried to teach it to us all, with his very words, through his very actions and deeds, and ultimately with his very life.

Rest in peace, Justen.
And may G-d have mercy on our souls.

Chapter 4

Barry

My Fall

This is for those who will listen
Listen very well … and I'll tell
    This story of my fall, I recall
    Didn't have to be … at all

Why must we die?
And cry
For our loved ones don't care
Never there … such despair

And the skyscrapers were tall
Taller than me … you see
    In the city, there were lonely nights
    And too many lights

When can I begin?
To give in
To someone I can trust
It's a must … such disgust

And the people were very cold,
Colder than ice … it's nice
    Take my advice, it's the place to grow old
    So the story is told

They had lied on a roll
To my heart ... and to my soul
I had lost, before I could even try
Not one of my dreams ... could I buy
She had been right, no one cared
I cried for help ... no one dared

And the noise was very loud,
Louder than sound ... I found.
Even on the ground, you'll be very proud
I'm going to kiss ... a cloud

Where, is she there?
Not fair
She's only on the phone
I don't own ... I'm alone

And the day was very dark
Darker than I ... don't cry
For even my, memories last forever
We'll always be together

Who, is that you?
Or someone new
I really cannot tell
All's not well ... I fell

Barry ended his life (or so he thought) by jumping off the balcony of the private dining suite at the Everest restaurant atop One Financial Plaza in Chicago, forty stories up.

Enough was enough ... he had given up.

A young man so full of hopes and dreams who came to the Windy City to seek his fortune in the stock market. With a more than moderate understanding of how the game was played from his five years at the Philadelphia Stock Exchange (PHLX), he thought he was ready for the big time. He wanted to play with the big boys.

Equities and futures were his forte, and he was beginning to understand how to hedge his bets on the commodities exchange as well. Working for a large brokerage firm as a trader on the floor, his ideas and brainstorms were always confiscated as the *intellectual property* of the company.

Once analyzed by the senior members, they were usually implemented quickly. Even though they were often *high risk,* they were almost always very lucrative and resulted in huge profits for the firm. Worst case, minimal gain ... but never a loss. The firm's notoriety and clientele grew steadily. The company's mutual fund portfolio on average consistently beat the composite growth index on all the major charts.

Barry was compensated with moderate raises in his salary but never with a percentage of what he was able to generate for the firm via his ingenious investment strategies. He had an innate ability to know when and what to buy, when and what to sell, when to invest, when to divest.

But he never received credit, recognition, or, more importantly, *appropriate proportional compensation* for his vision and creativity. He was sick of it. He was tired of being used. He wanted to call his own shots, manage his own set of funds, profit from his own ingenuity—or he wanted out.

You see, Barry had a hidden agenda. Unbeknownst to anyone, most of the money he made went to some charity somewhere—the United Way, the American Cancer Society, homeless shelters, and food banks. He spread his giving out to reach as many people as he could. As he saw it, it was the wealthy's responsibility to help those less fortunate.

All his contributions were anonymous, delivered in the form of a money order (no cash, less chance of theft) made out to the official name of the organization, via the US Postal Service with no return address. There were a lot of people in need, all over the world, so Barry needed to make as much money as he could. He wanted millions. He also knew that it was possible; he saw firsthand how rich people could get in the stock market. Why not him? Why not for his cause?

His opportunity came (again, or so he thought) when he got a call one day from a major firm in Chicago that needed a partner to manage a multimillion-dollar portfolio. Somehow his name had come up, and from the demeanor of the contact's conversation, Barry knew that they knew (there was always a *they* ... somewhere) that he was the brains behind his firm's success.

A partner? Wow. Was this it? Was he finally going to get his chance? Erica, his sweetheart of three years, didn't think so. She was more practical minded (as she was in her profession as a practical nurse) and wanted Barry to stay rooted, stay grounded, and stay home. Erica didn't want Barry to go chasing some *illusion* of equality in some distant city.

He could do that right here, with her by his side—there to congratulate him on the success of his ideas and to console him in his disappointment when he was denied the recognition he deserved.

Erica knew that what Barry was experiencing was unjust. But she accepted it as an extension of the injustice and exploitation that had plagued her people ever since their ancestors were brought to the Americas ... so many moons ago.

She also believed that we are given one chance at life and that we have to make the best of it. Play the hand that is dealt to you. No crying. No complaining.

So what if Barry didn't get full recognition on how to get rich using other people's money, who profited from the success of goods they didn't manufacture and services they didn't provide?

She understood that his gift was a blessing in that it provided him with a moderate income. Oh yeah, they would pay him, keep him well compensated, because they needed him—enough to afford him a decent living, a comfortable existence for them both. She was willing to accept this and build a life with him.

Barry drove a BMW 745 Li, not a Ford Focus. When they went out to eat, it was not Chick-fil-A but the Cheesecake Factory. They did not rent an apartment in Germantown but rather leased a condo on Rittenhouse Square. When they traveled, they flew first-class, and basically, they didn't want for anything.

Satisfied? Content? This Barry was not. He wanted more (you know why). He wanted to be treated fairly, viewed as an equal and allowed to get rich, just like all the other major players in the stock market. After all, they were his ideas (or were they?). It was his ingenious (or was it?). You see, Barry heard voices. Well, not really *voices* but a Voice—somewhat soothing and vaguely familiar.

For several years now, whenever he came to an impasse, that crucial decision point in fund portfolio strategic investment alignment that could result in a huge spread for a gain or a loss, Barry would ponder what to do, and the Voice would point him in the right direction. Always, without hesitation, Barry would advise his superiors to implement whatever the Voice had suggested. He had come to expect it. He had become dependent. When the Tylenol scare happened, every respected market analyst was advising sell. The Voice said:

Buy, Barry. Buy.

And so he advised. All his colleagues, the members of the firm on his level, rejected this insane suggestion. But the firm's senior partners had come to realize that no matter how ridiculous it may have seemed, they knew to trust Barry because Barry ... was always right. They accepted his recommendations without question, and to date, he had not let them down.

He would never explain his reasoning (because he couldn't) and would always walk out of the planning sessions after saying something stupid or funny like "A little bird told me so" or "I don't know ... just a hunch."

The firm grabbed up all the Tylenol shares they could get their greedy little hands on as the price kept falling and falling. In three months, when the stock value had nearly doubled from the price before the scare and seemed to level off, the firm unloaded a large amount of its equity and made a small fortune.

Similar events happened more and more frequently, and soon the firm consulted with Barry on every major decision. He always delivered because Barry would always wait for the Voice to guide him. And so it was for nearly five years—decisions, Barry, the Voice, recommendations, and prosperity. But Barry wanted more. He wanted what anyone would have wanted, which was to be recognized, to share equally in the profits, to be respected, to be accepted.

Of course, that never happened, and Barry became more and more frustrated. There were times when he thought to leave, to sign up with another brokerage house or investment firm or to start his own. But Barry knew enough about the game to know that his firm (well his current employer that is) was the biggest and the most respected, at least in Philly. Barry knew that if he signed up with someone else, he wouldn't earn as much (and couldn't give as much).

He also understood that if he tried to start his own company, his current firm would block his every move. They were powerful; they had all the right connections and all the right clients. So, when the call came from Chicago, another town, another playground, he couldn't resist. After all, the Chicago Mercantile Exchange, the *Merc,* was the largest options and futures market in the game, bigger than the NYSE and PHLX combined.

So, despite his darling Erica's warnings, concerns, and pleadings, he decided to take a chance and accepted the offer.

Bad move Barry ... too bad, so sad.

Cut to the chase.

Barry accepted the position in Chicago. The firm financed everything and set him up with a nice condo in the historic Edgewater Beach Apartments overlooking Lake Michigan on Lake Shore Drive. They increased his base salary by 20 percent and gave him the opportunity to make 30 percent on all profitable fund value increases. (The firm considered anything over 70 percent profitable.) It never happened.

In fact, the portfolio that Barry had control of consistently decreased in value. Barry was distraught; he didn't understand what was happening. One thing was clear: he needed the Voice to help him, to guide him into the right decisions. But the Voice never returned. He was all alone. The firm didn't like losing money, losing clients, and losing respect. They had to get rid of Barry with the quickness, so they set him up for the fall (in more ways than one).

His immediate supervisor called him into the office one morning, before the start of the trading day (Barry knew for sure that he was about to get the ax). He expressed that the firm was still behind him 100 percent and that they understood he was going through a rough patch. He told Barry that they had set up an appointment for him to meet with a senior investment analyst who could help get him back on track.

Barry was informed that the contact he was to meet with was a tall man who wore glasses, seemed to be in his early fifties, and he had some important data. The meeting itinerary was mailed to him via the US Postal Service, no forwarding address (Barry smiled when he got the letter), no email, no fax, and no Voice or text message.

Hmmm, now that's strange. In this digital age of communication? An actual letter? At this point, Barry didn't take notice and wouldn't have cared anyway. He was seriously (and soon to be literally) on edge. He was desperate.

He had absolutely no idea that the meeting was with a corporate official, who was the target of SEC investigation for insider trading. He had no idea that the meeting was being taped, that the information being disclosed was privileged, and that their communication was in fact criminal.

The very next day, Barry was arrested and charged with securities fraud, indictment and prosecution to follow. He was let go from the firm (now that they had just cause) and was left on his own. Barry was crushed; he was defeated.

Erica had said that if he left and went to Chicago, they were through, that she couldn't go with him and that she wouldn't wait for him to come to his senses. Erica truly loved Barry but believed with all her heart that he was making a big mistake. She begged him to stay. He went anyway.

Now what? What was he to do? He couldn't go back to Erica. He had burned his bridges with his old firm (they had heard the news and wouldn't touch him). He was about to go to prison. The case against him was solid.

Barry was caught on tape saying:

> Thank you for this information, Mr. Douglass. I'm sure that this data can be used to secure a profitable outcome for us both.

How could he be so stupid? How could he be so blind?

The *information* provided by Mr. Douglass outlined the actual closing dates of several major mergers and acquisitions that were *publicly pending* but were not officially finalized or approved ... but appeared to be headed in that direction. Barry knew that information of that nature, if accurate, if acted upon at the right time, could be *financially valuable* and could put him back on track with his firm in a big way.

He also knew that if the details of such information were not publicly available, it was clearly illegal.

After sipping the last drop of his rum and Coke, tears flowing from his eyes, his body shaking from heavy, heart-wrenching sobs that rocked his entire being, his very soul, Barry stepped onto the edge of the balcony and let himself fall.

On the way down, before he lost consciousness for lack of oxygen, Barry finally heard the Voice whisper:

It's all right, Barry. You're going to be all right.

Barry Stevenson was never seen or heard from by anyone ever again.

Chapter 5

The Young Ones

We Too … Have a Voice

Ours is a song unheard
It is a pretty song just the same
And although we may be young,
We have every right to play the game

Just like the beautiful butterfly
Fresh from its cocoon
We are and will be as lovely,
When we bloom as adults, real soon.

Listen to our guiding words
For in our thoughts there is much truth
From us you can also learn,
We are here … we are now … we are youth.

Do not decide all things for us
For we want and deserve a choice
Hear, respect, and try to understand us,
We too … have a Voice.

It is said that children have an innate sense of what is right and wrong. That they can tell the good from the bad. That they can sense evil. It is believed by some that children's hearts are pure, free from the boundaries of hate, jealousy, and envy, that they see the world from a different perspective, with a different lens.

Children are so full of joy, wonder, and surprise. Hope and the promise of tomorrow brighten all their days and allow them to dream of a beautiful future. It is only the passing of time that begins to erode their layers of love. As they come in contact with the evils of the world, with each disappointment and act of treachery that they experience, they begin to realize and understand that something is wrong ... something is not right.

COTAT, as they were called, *Children of Today and Tomorrow,* refused to accept this slow deterioration of life as the *norm* for the human experience. They were a youth group with a purpose; they were on a mission. They went from neighborhood to neighborhood, from city to city, and *preached* their message of love to the world. COTAT was an improvisational teen drama group. They would brainstorm scenarios from life, develop characters, and put on skits.

After each scene, the actors and actresses would stay in character and interact with the audience. Then they would come out of character and introduce themselves. All the COTAT players were collectively chosen and accepted by the group, very carefully, very selectively.

Members had to be free spirits, free of hate and malice, with a desire and passion to want to spread the light of love. The team was very special. Members of COTAT were a tight-knit bunch. Players came and went, but this last three years, a core group formed, solid as a rock and friends for life.

Jessica (fifteen)

Bubbly and full of laughter. Her main character was Ebony, a dark child who always found herself in some sort of trouble: a pregnant teen, afraid to tell her parents; a young girl who wanted to impress those who she thought were her friends and the boy she liked by trying drugs ...

Terrance (seventeen)

A dark-haired lad with freckles. The studious one. His characters were always close to his real personality, the one in the group who you could always turn to, who always seemed to have the right answers ...

Emily (sixteen)

A quiet child with a beautiful smile and a loving nature. Her characters were always in stark contrast to her personality; they were dark and sinister. She always chose to be the antagonist in the scene: an abusive mother, a jealous friend, the bad seed. She wanted to be good at playing these roles so she could engage the audience and hopefully reach someone, hoping it would help them to see the problems that this type of behavior caused. She knew that there were people out there struggling with these issues, and she wanted to help them.

Brandon (eighteen)

A shy, withdrawn lad who in real life stayed in the background, never wanting to draw attention to himself ... a true loner. But on stage, he was on fire and full of energy. The other characters could always count on Brandon to keep things moving, to liven things up when the drama got a little stale. Being a member of COTAT was like therapy for him; it would undoubtedly help him to develop into the fine young man he was destined to become.

This was the core of the troop, the center of the group. Other players would come and go, but these troopers always set the tone and the pace. They were guided by their mentor and chaperone on outings, Mr. Davis (a tall man who wore glasses and seemed to be in his early fifties).

On a Saturday trip to Norristown to visit a community rec center and put on a skit about the dangers of STDs and drug usage for a group of local teens, their bus never arrived at its destination.

As the bus climbed a steep, winding curve, the driver lost control (primarily because he was speeding). The vehicle listed sharply to the left, crashed through the barrier, and began tumbling down the hillside. The passengers (screaming) were tossed around like clothes in a dryer. Upon hitting a large rock, the fuel line erupted, and the bus burst into flames.

A rolling, bright yellow tomb of fire that finally came to rest at the bottom of the hill sealing the fate of all thirty-two passengers—thirty-three people including the careless driver.

When the authorities, news teams, and horrified on lookers arrived at the scene of the broken, strewn wreckage all over the hillside, they also sadly observed the mutilated, charred remains of children. Twenty-seven young, innocent lives were lost that day along with two adults ... one innocent, one guilty.

Although the hillside was scoured inch by inch, the remains of Terrance, Jessica, Brandon, Emily, and Mr. Davis were never found.

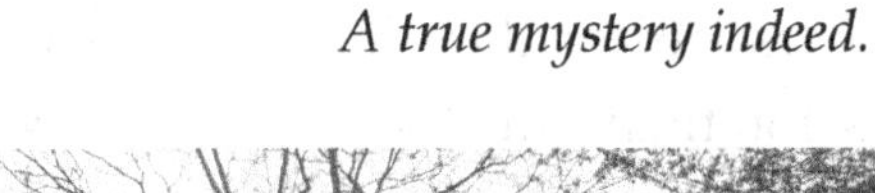

A true mystery indeed.

Chapter 6

All in all, 120 people disappeared in 2003 from various walks of life, at different ages, from diverse cultures, from all over the globe. In some cases, it appeared that they met a tragic end—a violent accident, an act of terrorism. In most cases, they started out their days in their normal routines but never came home. In all cases, they were never really injured; no harm came to them in any way.

The illusion of despair for their loved ones and for their families was for them, all too real. There were mysterious disappearances, unexplained circumstances, and in every case, there was a constant element … the Voice. In the last moments of what they thought was the end of their lives, was the tall man who wore glasses and appeared to be in his early fifties. A force was at work here. An unseen presence. These people, these souls represented the essence of the good that could still be found in human existence.

They were indicative of what mankind could be … should be. Their lives spoke of kindness, compassion, caring, and concern for others. They had been abducted, taken from their loved ones for a purpose … for the greater good. But by whom? How? Why? They each had a gift, something unique to offer mankind. And now it was time for phase 2 of the *plan* to be set in motion. For time was a precious commodity that was slipping away from them all.

Phase 2

Awareness

Chapter 7

The Awakenings

8:30 a.m.

Wake up, Melissa. Wake up.

It was the seventh day, and Melissa still relied on the Voice to wake her up. She had no fear. She accepted this new existence for her life, for the time being. Somehow she knew; she felt certain that she was in no danger.

Melissa: (always speaking in a calm and serene tone, never apprehensive, never angry):

Good morning, and how are you today?

We are fine, thank you.

Why do you keep saying we? All I ever hear is you.

There are others.

When am I going to get the chance to talk to them? Maybe they will have some answers.

Soon, Melissa. Soon you will know everything. Please take your shower and have your breakfast.

Her *quarters* (for lack of a better term) were very nice, all the amenities one could ask for—a plush, comfortable queen-size bed in a bedroom filled with all sorts of the things she liked but never had the time (or the funds) to acquire. Satin sheets, fluffy pillows, a canopy. There were dressers filled with comfortable clothes, all her favorites. There was a full bathroom that had a walk-in, smoked-glass shower and an old Victorian tub.

Melissa took showers in the morning and long, luxurious, hot bubble baths at night. She had all her favorite soaps, ointments, lotions, and perfumes. Everything was right there for her (towels, bath clothes, velour robes, etc.). There was also a den, a kitchen, and an exercise room. In the den, there was a comfortable leather couch, a La-Z-Boy ® recliner, and a posh love seat. There were bookshelves that contained what seemed to be vintage copies of all her favorite books, ones that she had read and ones that she had always wanted to.

Mounted on the wall, was a forty-four-inch flat-screen TV that was programmed with every movie and every Cable or TV show that Melissa knew of. All the films were full-length features, and all the TV shows had every episode (with no commercials). The display was crystal clear in what Melissa could only describe as super high definition, (whatever that was) but it had the best picture and sound quality she had ever seen or heard anywhere.

She could watch anything at any time, but there were never any news channels or programs. The *dwelling* had no clocks anywhere.

Melissa's cell phone and watch were nowhere to be found. The rooms, all of them, were decorated to her taste, to the finest detail in every way—color, style, feel, texture, and décor—but there no windows or doors. There seemed to be no way out.

Every morning, after she took her shower and got dressed, when she went into the kitchen, breakfast would be waiting for her ... always freshly prepared, hot and delicious. It was like this for lunch and dinner also. The kitchen had no cupboards, refrigerator, stove, countertop, or appliance. Just a nice glass table and a comfortable chair for dining. Where did all the meals come from? Who was preparing them? Where did the dirty dishes go?

Melissa never saw anyone, never heard anything. *How do they know what I like to eat?* The exercise room was a dream, fully equipped with a sauna and an Olympic-sized swimming pool with six lanes. Everything was always so clean and fresh and smelled so good.

The Voice was always there with her; it seemed to be all around her, talking to her whenever she wanted to talk, taking orders for snacks, lunch, and dinner. But it never answered any questions or gave up any information that would explain what had happened, why she was here, and the most important question of all ...

Was her dear son, her beloved Michael, okay?

But today was different. Today she would learn more than she ever wanted to know. Today she would become *aware*.

After a modest lunch of tuna fish on pita with raspberry iced tea and fresh pineapple, Melissa went to her den to watch the rest of *Set It Off* with Jada Pickett-Smith, Kimberly Elise, and cast. She had started watching it two nights ago but fell asleep in the La-Z-Boy ®. When the Voice woke her up the next morning, she was in her bed.

She climbed back into the La-Z-Boy ®, reclined, and issued a command to pick the movie up where she had left off. There was no remote control. The Voice had instructed Melissa that all she had to do was say what she wanted, and her wishes would be granted (to a point of course).

Melissa always had classical Beethoven playing in every room, all the time (except when she was watching a movie or show).

You can finish watching the movie later, Melissa.
Now it is time.

Time for what?

For you to receive some of the answers.
To your questions.

Okay, I'll play along. For starters, is Michael okay? Can I see him?

Michael is fine. As well as can be expected without you there with him. He is in no danger.
Before we continue, I must explain to you how our question and answer sessions will work.

You may ask any question that you like. I will always answer if the information is within the realm of what you can know. In time, you will have all the answers to all your questions. Your knowledge and understanding must come in Awareness Stages, of which there are three. When we feel that you are ready for the next Stage, we will guide your revelations accordingly. The answer to your second question is no. You cannot see your son now, but when the time comes, if you so choose, you will be reunited with Michael.

Tears welled in Melissa's eyes, and she felt a lump in her throat.

> Okay, okay. I believe that Michael is okay. I don't think that you would do all of this for me and then hurt my son. Okay, give me a minute please ... I need a minute.

Take all the time that you need.

Melissa (after taking a deep breath and closing her eyes for a minute):

> I want a writing pad and a pen so that I can jot down everything we talk about. I don't want to miss anything.

That will not be necessary. I will provide you with whatever information you need, at any time that you like, as long as it is within your current Awareness Stage.

> Okay. Let's do this. Am I alone? Are there other people around, like me, somewhere, just as confused as I am?

There are 649 other people who were removed from their lives. You are number 650.

> Who are you? Why don't you show yourself? Who gave you the right to take me from my Michael? To take any of us!

You are upset and highly emotional. In this state, you're Awareness cannot continue. Only when you are calm, when you can think rationally. Only then can we continue.

The view screen lit up, and *Set It Off* continued.

> No wait! Come back! I want to continue, please ... please ...

The Voice didn't return. Not that day or evening. After a crying spell, Melissa watched the rest of the movie (which had automatically paused until she was ready to continue). After the movie, Melissa watched some nature shows (to help keep her in touch with the outside world). Then she took a nap.

12:06 p.m.

Melissa awoke on her own. When she fell asleep, she was lying on the couch fully dressed. She awoke in comfortable lingerie, in her bed. She got up and put on a robe. Upon entering the kitchen, she found a grilled cheese sandwich with tomato and pepper-jack on wheat bread, a bowl of tomato bisque soup, and a tall glass of homemade iced tea flavored with ginseng and honey. Everything was delicious.

That afternoon, she worked out, took a swim, sat in the sauna for a while, then went back to her La-Z-Boy ® and watched two more movies, *Gladiator* and *Brave Heart.* Mel Gibson was one of her favorite actors. Dinner that evening was baked salmon, asparagus, brown rice with corn, and a glass of white wine.

Melisa realized that the Voice wouldn't return until the morning. She promised herself that she would keep it together next time. She wanted answers. Whatever this was, whatever game was being played, she would see it through to the end. She would do her very best so that she could be there again for Michael.

... but when the time comes, if you so choose,
you will be reunited with Michael ...

Those words echoed in Melissa's mind and heart like a favorite song. She would let this drive her, give her the energy to endure whatever was to come. *I mean how bad could it be? Look at this place!*

As she lay down that evening, a quiet sense of calm came over her, and she closed her eyes in peace.

Rest well, Melissa. Rest well.

And so she did.

8:36 a.m.

Wake up, Melissa. Wake up.

Breakfast this morning consisted of French toast with blueberries and ginger, coffee, orange juice, and one egg over easy.

How are you feeling today, Melissa?

> Better thank you. I'll be ready to continue today.

That's very good.

Melissa decided not to rush it. She gave herself time to calm her nerves and settle her emotions.

She believed that her progression through these Awareness Stages (as the Voice called them) depended entirely on her ability to accept and make the best of her new reality. But it wasn't easy. Again, Melissa's strength and solace would come from Michael. The mere thought of their anticipated reunion would help to fortify her resolve and help her to *keep it together.*

After breakfast, Melissa went to the den (the love seat and some fluffy pillows this time) and watched another movie, *Heat,* the classic thriller with Al Pacino and Robert De Niro. The scene in the restaurant where Lt. Vincent Hanna talked with Neil McCauley was legendary. She liked shoot-'em-ups, but they had to be wrapped around good drama and superb acting.

2:10 p.m.

After the movie, she ordered a virgin strawberry daiquiri and some beer-battered chicken fingers with honey mustard on the side. She began to think about how she would approach this next session. She decided to ask questions that were pertinent to getting her out of there. No judgments, no accusations. If she felt that it was too much, she would take a break, regain her composure, and then continue.

Melissa prepared her mind to hear anything. It was obvious that whoever they were (the mysterious powers behind this constant Voice), they were in control. Circumstances notwithstanding, her time here (wherever here was) was pleasant, comfortable, and relaxing.

It was almost like a well-deserved vacation, one that she never could have afforded in a million years.

Melissa (thinking to herself):

Okay, tuts, let's get this show on the road. You're not going to get anywhere by just sitting here.

Melissa changed into some comfortable clothes, plopped into the La-Z-Boy ® (her favorite chair), swiveled it in front of the view screen, took a deep breath, said a quiet prayer, and addressed the Voice.

Okay, I'm ready to begin.

Very good.

So, refresh my memory again. What exactly are these three Awareness Stages? What are the parameters and rules?

You may ask any question that you like. All information will be given to you, if the answers fall within your current Awareness Stage. Stage 1 involves understanding why you are here, you along with the others. Stage 2 involves reaching an understanding of what you must do if you decide to stay here or return to your lives. Stage 3 is only for those who decide to stay. It is the Awareness Stage that we hope you all will reach.

Melissa did not respond right away. She took some time to let all of what she just heard sink in. There was some plan here, something that she felt was much bigger than her individual existence but involved the collective *captives* and maybe beyond. Now she was curious; now she was interested in really knowing what the hell was going on.

How long have I been here?

Three years, two months and a day.

Mild shock started to creep into her psyche, but she fought it off. *Calm down, Melissa. Calm down.*

It's 2006?

Yes. June 12 to be exact.

But I only woke up seven days ago. That's right … right?

Yes.

Okay, Melissa, get a grip. Where was I for three years? Here?

Yes, we had you in stasis.

The view screen came on, showing a room in which there was some sort of chamber. The view zoomed, and Melissa clearly saw herself lying in the chamber, unconscious or asleep.

I was in there for three years?

Melissa felt her arms, her legs. She stood up.

Wait, my muscles … no atrophy. I feel fine … I–

Melissa stopped. Something occurred to her that she didn't realize before.

She jumped up, ran to the bathroom, and stripped naked. She looked at her body, her face. She examined her teeth. After about twenty minutes, she got dressed and went back to the den. She sat down and took another deep breath. The view screen was still on and still showed her in the chamber.

> How did you do it? My cellular mitosis has not changed. All my scars, remnants of my previous injuries are gone. I have all my teeth. Explain.

You have been restored to perfect health. Every aspect of your physical condition is that of a healthy twenty-seven-year-old human female.

> This is impossible. Are you some sort of advanced scientific team of doctors or something?

Melissa's mind suddenly flashed back to Alicyn and all the other children of the world who were stricken with deadly diseases.

> You have the power to cure anything, to heal anyone from any type of disease, infection, or injury? You can reconstruct human tissue? Bone? Brain matter?

Yes, Melissa, yes. Your complete restoration is very real. There is absolutely nothing wrong with you in any way.

An examination by any doctor, in any hospital in the world, would reveal a woman in perfect health. There isn't even any evidence that you have had a child.

Melissa's mind began to race. She didn't know where to begin, what to ask next. There was so much she wanted to know, needed to know. *Get a grip, Melissa. You do want to get to stage 2, don't you?*

> A cold glass of orange-pineapple juice please, no ice.

As you wish, it is on the table, in the kitchen.

Melissa's went to the kitchen, retrieved her drink, and came back and sat down. The beverage would help to steady her as she continued.

> All right, all right. I don't know how you did it, and right now, that's not important. I'll ask those questions later. Okay, are all the other people like me?

Yes, Melissa. Each of them has been restored to perfect health for the age when they were taken. They all are in Stage 1 Awareness.

> Are they here, in this place, complex, whatever you call it? Can I meet them?

The other 649 individuals who were taken are spread out all over the planet.

Your collective of sixty-four will be united and linked via the view screen systems as the whole group moves into Stage 2 Awareness. Your immediate group consists of eight individuals. Initially, you will communicate via the view screens. Become familiar with one another. Then you can meet in person.

Were we all taken three years ago?

No, Melissa. The abductions started in 2003. The last group was taken only eight days ago. We took each of you at a special moment in your lives. At a time when it seemed that all hope was lost.

So, are they all alone like me? Surrounded with all the comforts of life, except other people?

No, Melissa. At your location, you are the only one who is alone. Yes, they were all provided with nourishment. They all have been comforted to suit their needs as well.

Who are they?

The view screen changed to show the rest of the abductees at Melissa's location, and the Voice said their first names only. Celeste, Justen, Barry and the young ones, Jessica, Terrance, Emily, and Brandon. When Melissa saw the young ones, tears welled in her eyes again.

You took children, you took children …

Yes, Melissa.

Why? Why are we all here? What do you want from us?

The answers to those questions will come in time. They will be answered collectively via the view screens. When you all are ready. When you have accepted your realities.

Okay, okay. Why am I the only one who is alone?

You, Melissa, are the most emotional. You needed this time alone. Before you could meet with the others.

Melissa agreed with that … no arguments there.

Is there something different about us, about all the others who were taken?

In time, all of you will accept your realities. True, you were all abducted. Taken from your daily lives, from your loved ones. You will learn that each of you was chosen. Each of you is special; you have collectively and as individuals unique qualities that are the very best that mankind has to offer.

Melissa was not flattered at all.

Okay, so we are all good people. So what? By whose authority and by what right did you forcibly and under such duress bring us here and to the other locations?

That, you will understand in time.

Okay, so now what?

It is almost time for you to speak with the others. In two days.

All right. So, until then, it's business as usual?

Melissa had another question. But before she could ask it, she had to prepare herself for the answer. Her emotions were somewhat under control, and she wanted to keep them that way, but she had to know. She needed to know.

Our families, all our families, what do they think happened to us?

Your families have accepted their losses. They have moved on.

Melissa thought, but didn't say out loud:

You bastards, who the hell do you think you are?

So, whatever this is, whatever this is all about ... you really believe it is worth it?

Yes, Melissa, it is.

I think I'll go lie down for a while.

As you wish.

For the next two days, Melissa didn't ask any more questions. She just relaxed and tried not to think about anything at all. She just went through her normal routine of freshly prepared meals, hot showers, long baths, good workouts, La-Z-Boy ® movies, and superb shut-eye.

What she was about to learn, about the whole order of things, would shock her to the core. As bad as things were, (being traumatically abducted, being separated from her precious Michael for three years, or so she was told), things were about to get much worse.

Wake up, Celeste. Wake up.

Celeste was a little dizzy at first, but soon her head cleared, and she opened her eyes to find a little girl looking down at her.

She's awake! She's awake!

Jessica ran to tell the others. They were playing a round of PS2 Space Invaders as a team and were on the last wave. Emily and Brandon dropped their control pads, jumped up, and were about to run in to see her.

Terrance (always the Voice of reason):

Wait!

Terrance had finished his stage 1 awareness in one day; it took the others over a week. Terrance had been awakened first. Then the rest of the group (Jessica, Brandon, and Emily) all at once. Their *quarters* were plush and complete to taste (of course). They each had their own rooms with private bathrooms, filled with all the things they liked, and they were connected to and shared common dining, exercise, and audio/visual entertainment areas.

The Voice communicated only with Terrance. He accepted his reality right away.

You're going to have to explain to the others, Terrance. You have to help them to understand. They will listen to you; they always have.

Okay, when can I see them?

Let us use the view screens at first. Then, one by one you can all be reunited.

You mean when they're no longer afraid.

That's right, Terrance. You are very perceptive. Initially they will be afraid. I will help you to reassure them that everything is okay. I will speak only to you, inside your mind, like this …

The last two words were only audible inside Terrance's head. He smiled.

This is cool.

Now when you want to talk to me, don't speak your words out loud. Just think them, and I will hear you.

Terrance (thinking):

Will the others be able to hear you too?

No, Terrance, not just yet. Only you.

This is tight. What's your name?

What do you want to call me?

How about Steve? No wait … let's use Joshua!

Okay, Joshua it is. At any time, you can talk to me. I will always be here to answer your questions. About anything at all. When the others are ready, together you and I will help them to understand what has happened. Together we will guide them on what they must do. Do you think you can do that?

Yeah, I can do it.

Thank you, Terrance.

We're on some kind of mission, aren't we?

Yes, Terrance. A very important one. You and the others were chosen to help us.

> You have to help me. Just let me know what to say, when I should say it, and I'll take care of the rest.

Terrance liked his new role. It gave him a sense of power. Joshua completed Terrance's Stage 1 Awareness in a matter of hours. One by one, Joshua and Terrance helped Jessica, Emily, and Brandon complete Stage 1 Awareness in a little over a week. They were all brought together and began living as a group, two weeks before they were informed of Celeste. Joshua coached Terrance on how to prepare the group for Celeste.

Terrance:

> We shouldn't crowd her. She's already going to be in shock as it is. Jessica, did she see you?

Jessica:

> I think so. She opened her eyes.

Terrance:

You should go back to her room by yourself. When she asks, tell her that she is okay and that everything is going to be all right. When she calms down, tell her that there are some other kids here and that we would like to see her.

Jessica:

Okay, I'll go.

Jessica headed back to Celeste's room.

Celeste:

Stacey! Oh my G-d! Where's my baby?

Jessica:

It's okay, Ms. Celeste. You're gonna be okay.

Celeste:

Where's Stacey? Am I …

She sat up and noticed her surroundings, plush room … comfortable bed. She checked herself and realized that she was not injured and felt no pain whatsoever.

Celeste:

Am I in a hospital? Who are you?

Jessica:

My name is Jessica. Pleased to meet you.

Jessica extended her hand, which Celeste took and squeezed very gently in both of her own. She didn't let go.

Celeste (a little calmer now):

> Hello, Jessica. I have a daughter named Stacey. Do you know where she is? Is she here with me? Is she okay?

At that moment, as if on cue, Terrance, Emily, and Brandon came into room and gathered around Celeste.

Terrance:

> Hello, Ms. Celeste. My name is Terrance. This is Emily, and this is Brandon.

Emily and Brandon in unison:

> Hi.

Terrance (continuing):

> Ms. Celeste, Stacey didn't make it.

As if choreographed in a final rehearsal of a Broadway play, the group waited in suspended animation. Celeste just sat there with a blank look on her face. A tiny tear trickled down her face. Then she closed her eyes, hung her head low, and began to cry. The group converged on her and embraced her with a protective hug. Celeste never let go of Jessica's hand. Emily gently stroked her head, and Brandon kissed her on the forehead.

In that moment of grief and utter despair for Celeste, a bond was formed between her and the young ones ... especially with Jessica. They sat there for about fifteen minutes, not speaking, just comforting Celeste as her sobs slowly began to subside, rocking with her gently back and forth.

Celeste:

> Do you all know what happened?

Terrance (guided by Joshua):

> Yes, Ms. Celeste. Hey guys, go make Ms. Celeste some hot chocolate and a corned beef special on wheat toast with a pickle and let me talk to her for a while.

The group members took turns kissing Celeste on the cheek, then left for the kitchen together.

Jessica:

> I'll be back Ms. Celeste.

They headed out, leaving Celeste alone with Terrance.

Celeste:

> How did you know what I like?

Terrance:

> We know all about you Ms. Celeste, all about you, Stacey, your husband, Milton, Ms. Sarah ... everything.

Somehow, for some reason that she couldn't quite put her finger on, Celeste wasn't startled or upset at this revelation.

And they did know. After all the young ones completed Stage 1 Awareness, they were told that their first assignment would be to help (Ms.) Celeste. They gathered around the view screens as Terrance narrated the story of Celeste's life. Off and on, the girls cried. They saw everything ... up to and including the plane crash that killed Stacey and all the others, except Celeste and the tall man with the glasses.

During Stage 1 Awareness for Terrance, it was revealed to him by Joshua just who that man was and what part he played in all their lives. You see, Terrance was informed not only about Celeste and her life but also about Justen, Barry, and Melissa.

The Voice shared everything with Terrance, because Terrance had accepted it all as a new reality and was determined to make the best of it.

Terrance (sitting on the bed next to Celeste and taking both of her hands in his):

> Ms. Celeste, I know this is hard for you, but you have to be strong. All of us here, Jessica, Emily, Brandon, and myself included, we have all lost loved ones. And there are others, many others.

Celeste (her hands began to tremble):

> Where am I? What is this place? I was on that plane as it was going down. I remember my little girl screaming. I was right there with her. If we crashed, if she died, then why am I still alive? Why am I not hurt? Look at me! There is absolutely nothing wrong with me!

Terrance (he could feel her pulse racing):

> You were saved. Do you remember seeing a tall man with glasses sitting in first class with you?

Celeste:

> Yes, I remember him.

Terrance:

> He saved you. He is a paratrooper. That day, he had on a body chute. When they travel as civilians, they always wear one. When the plane went down, he popped open an emergency hatch, grabbed you, and jumped before it crashed. You had already passed out.

Celeste:

> I remember a Voice, my special Voice, telling me that I was going to be all right. Was that him?

Terrance:

Yes Ms. Celeste. He has been with you for a long time, hasn't he?

Celeste (beginning to cry again):

Yes.

Terrance:

Ms. Celeste, there were over 120 people on that plane. He couldn't stop the plane from crashing, and he couldn't save everyone. Not even Stacey. But he had to save you, Ms. Celeste.

Celeste:

Why me? Why me?

Terrance:

You are special, Ms. Celeste. We all are. That's why we are all here, together. He saved all of us. Come, let's get you something to eat. Afterward, we can all sit down, and we'll tell you everything that we know. Okay?

Celeste:

Okay—Terrance ... right?

Terrance:

Yes, Ms. Celeste, that's right.

They got up and went into the kitchen where the others were waiting for them. Each of them had their own special lunch dish. Unlike the place where Melissa was, the young ones and Celeste enjoyed a fully stocked pantry, fully equipped kitchen, and an expansive outdoor garden with every vegetable imaginable. They had several refrigerators and freezers that were always stocked with all their favorites. They prepared all their own meals.

They had all waited for Celeste and Terrance. The group sat down and ate together. For the next two weeks, the young ones, led by Terrance (and Joshua), helped to guide Celeste through Stage 1 Awareness. When they were ready, they learned of Melissa. On the second day of the third week, Celeste, the young ones, and Melissa were all together.

Melissa:

> I wish I had stayed by myself. Then I wouldn't have to cook. I loved having all my favorite dishes just appear out of thin air ... just like magic. And no dishes to wash either.

Celeste:

> That's cause you're lazy.

Emily (laughing):

> It's okay, Ms. Melissa. I'll cook for you. I like cooking.

Melissa:

> That's because you're a sweet little girl.
> Never mind Ms. mean ole Celeste.

Emily:

> I'll cook for everybody. I love cooking!

It was very good for Melissa to be around people again, especially around children. Although she still missed her Michael dearly, the young ones made her feel good inside. Just being around them was soothing. The bond between Celeste and Jessica grew stronger every day. They were inseparable. They even slept together. After two weeks, Terrance told the group that they had another mission of sorts. These days, the Voice was not audible to anyone.

Melissa and Celeste could have their own private or collective conversations with Joshua (they all called the Voice by this name now), and they heard in their minds all of Joshua's communications with Terrance. It was explained to them (and they agreed) that it was better if Jessica, Emily, and Brandon were guided by Terrance. Their new assignment was to watch the Stage 1 Awareness processes of Barry and then Justen.

Barry would join the group once he was ready, and then the group would watch as Barry assisted Justen. Terrance let everyone know that it was better if Justen was assisted by Barry. Once Justen had finished his Stage 1 Awareness, the entire group would go through Stage 2 Awareness together.

Melissa wanted to get back to Michael in the worst way, but for some reason, she dreaded Stage 2 Awareness.

Melissa thought of Joshua's chilling revelation:

Stage 2 Awareness involves reaching an understanding of what you must do if you decide to stay here or return to your lives.

What on earth could be so grave? What could possibly exist that would present a choice between here and Michael? Even though she understood clearly that there was something here that was bigger than her, bigger than Michael, she was a little afraid of what that might be ... afraid of what she might choose.

Barry's Stage 1 Awareness went well, and he joined the group in four days. Terrance told them of the special parameters that would exist for Justen. Barry and Justen would both hear Joshua in their minds but had to speak with him out loud. When Justen would realize that he and Barry could hear the same thing, the same Voice, it would help with his progress.

Wake up, Justen. Wake up.

Justen sat up immediately. He checked his wounds, which weren't there.

He thought:

Am I unconscious? Am I dreaming?

No, Justen, you are awake, and yes, your wounds are gone.

Justen stood up, stripped naked, and thoroughly examined himself from head to toe. No aspect of this was censored from the group as they watched. Melissa and Celeste looked at each other briefly but said nothing.

There are mirrors in the bathroom to your left.

Justen went into the bathroom and examined himself further. Everything was in order, except he could not find one single scar on his body. He had no blemishes on his skin, he had all his teeth, which were healthy, and he felt absolutely fine. Justen knew that he had been shot, twice.

He clearly remembered Agent Wilson fixing him up. Where were the scars? Where were the stitches? Were they able to get both bullets out? He didn't have his glasses on or his contacts, yet as far as he could tell, he could see better now than he could in his entire life.

Well, I can say this you sure have a crackpot team of doctors and surgeons.

Justen got dressed and examined the bathroom. It was exquisite, complete with all his favorite amenities: soap, lotion, cologne.

The walk-in glass shower had a header with a detachable handheld nozzle, and the towels and face cloths were plush.

Justen thought to himself:

> *Okay, I'll play this to the end. Let's see where this goes.*

This is not a game, Justen. This is no sort of mind jerk, as you would call it.

Justen (angered):

> I don't know how you were able to read my thoughts, and I don't really care to know right now. But if I'm going to cooperate, then you do something for me:
>
> *Stay out of my head!*
>
> Even if you can tell, don't read my thoughts. At least give me the illusion of having some sort of control, even though it's obvious that I do not. Comprende?!

Understood.

Melissa smiled inside. She liked the way Justen was handling things. He may have been totally afraid, but he wasn't about to show it. He was cool, calm, and collected with a touch of spice.

Justen reminded Melisa of Stephen. For a moment, her mind flashed back to an evening out with her beloved husband.

They had just come from the theatrical debut of *Gladiator,* the Russell Crowe, Oscar-winning classic, and were on their way for a bite to eat, totally mesmerized by the epic saga.

Walking hand in hand, they cut through an alley and were accosted by three knife-wielding thugs demanding cash, jewelry ... whatever.

Bad move. Too bad, so sad ... for them.

In the blink of an eye, Stephen had disarmed and disabled all three, without hesitation, totally confident, and in total control. In no time flat, the young wannabe hoodlums were lying on the ground in dazed stupors, nursing injuries (a concussion for one and all with broken bones to boot).

Stephen calmly reassured Melissa that everything would be all right, that they should call and wait for the police in order to give a full report and to make sure that none of *goons* tried to limp away. Later that evening when Melissa inquired about Stephen's newly revealed *abilities,* he explained that he had to keep his martial arts skills a secret. Over time, he had discovered that people would react differently to him once they found out. Sharing it was more trouble than it was worth.

He also shared with her that his training had given him an overwhelming sense of confidence and self-control that transcended to other areas of his life. He convinced Melissa to start training herself, and so she did.

The only time Melissa had an opportunity to demonstrate her self-defense prowess was when she was subdued by the tall man with the glasses, in the cramped confines of an SUV, trying to save a little girl's life. That time, she was totally ineffective.

Something about Justen's calm sense of determination not to let this newfound *reality* get the best of him reminded her of Stephen.

Justen walked back into what he determined was the living room of his new *residence* and sat down in a comfortable arm chair. He gazed around the room ... plush, cozy. It had a wall-to-wall library (which he later discovered contained authentic journals, documents, and top-secret official government reports of every skirmish, coup d'état, conflict, and war that there ever was, all over the globe, throughout all recorded history) but with no visible doors or windows.

Justen, closing his eyes, thought to himself, not caring if they could read his thoughts or not:

> *Okay, I'll play along ... see this through till the end, but I'll keep my head, stay focused.*

Justen had been through a lot. He had survived a lot where others had perished. Through every trauma, Justen had remained composed before, during, and after. Everyone appreciated having him around because he was consistently that cool, calm, collected and level-headed dude who would always find a way.

He came up with the best way to defuse a situation, resolve a conflict, or get them out of a pickle. This was different. There was something unusual about his present dilemma—something eerily not real and beyond his comprehension that was starting to unnerve him in the worst way.

For the first time since he could remember, all the way back to the days of roaming the hills of Montana with his father and brothers, he couldn't *assess* the situation. He *wasn't* in control. Justen was afraid.

Justen (in the calmest, most even-toned Voice that he could muster):

> What do I call you?

Joshua will do.

> Okay, Joshua, in very plain English, complete but to the point, I want to know everything—who you are, how and why I am here, where I am and what you want with me, the truth and all of it, right here and right now.

At that precise moment, Melissa just thought—it came from nowhere but from deep within:

Melissa:

> *Joshua, let me do it. I know that you said Barry would assist Justen, but let me, please?*

Melissa looked at Barry, who just smiled and nodded in agreement. Joshua already knew; he had already spoken to Barry.

Mellissa, speak to Justen in your mind. He will hear your Voice out loud. I will guide you, and the group will hear everything.

Melissa:

> Hello, Justen. My name is Melissa.

Justen:

> What part of the game is this? Where did Joshua go?

Melissa:

> No game, Justen. I'm here, just like you. There are others, even children. We were all brought here against our will, but we're okay. No harm has come to us, and no harm will come to you.

Justen:

> Where are you? I want to see you.

Joshua told Melissa where to go, and in a minute, she was walking through a doorway and appeared in Justen's *living room.* Justen stood up as Melissa approached him, dressed in blue jeans and a Chicago University sweatshirt.

Melissa:

> Please sit.

Justen moved over to a sofa that was in the room and sat down. Melissa sat next to him and instinctively took his hand.

Melissa:

> I don't know everything, none of us do, but I'll tell you what I do know. Then you'll only be in the dark as much as the rest of us are.

Justen:

> Okay.

Melissa broke it down. She told Justen of her personal experience, of how she had come to be in this place. She told him of the others and their stories. She explained to the best of her ability about the three Awareness Stages and everything Joshua had explained to her. After she had finished her forty-five-minute monologue, there was a full moment of silence.

Justen (smiling):

> This was better hearing it from you. Thank you. Somehow, I don't know why, but I believe you. I don't understand all of it, but I know you are sincere ... I can feel it. Was this your idea or Joshua's?

Melissa (smiling back):

> It was mine. I don't know, but initially Joshua said that Barry would initiate you. I just wanted to ... I just needed to talk to you. I guess I felt that it would help to make this more real for me, to help someone else.

Justen:

> You did just fine. Is there anything to eat around here?

Melissa (laughing):

> Well, having an appetite is good.

Joshua (audible to everyone):

Please, come into the dining area.

They got up together and found their way into the *dining room* where the entire group was waiting for them. Jessica ran over to Justen and gave him a tight hug. Celeste began to cry. One by one, each of them went over and introduced themselves to Justen. Emily and Celeste embraced him, while Barry, Terrance, and Brandon shook his hand.

Melissa:

> Well, here we are, one big happy family.

Emily had directed the preparation of a feast. With Joshua's help in identifying each of the group member's favorite dishes, she guided Terrance, Jessica, and Brandon in cooking a wonderful meal. Barry and Celeste had set the table, while the young ones gathered the serving dishes. Melissa and Justen just sat there like guests of honor, sipping glasses of sparkling apple cider.

Out of nowhere, the piano rhythmic melodies of the Bob James CD *Dancing on the Water* began playing (one of Justen's favorite compilations). Melissa led them in grace, and they began to dine.

Barry:

> I hope this is not the meal before the slaughter.

The adults laughed (all except Justen), and the young ones giggled.

I assure you, it is not.

Everyone turned toward the doorway, and there he stood, the tall man with the glasses, in his trench coat, Joshua in the flesh (or so it would appear). No one spoke. Joshua remained in the doorway.

Joshua:

You are all ready. Terrance, it would appear that Justen has broken your record for Stage 1 Awareness.

Joshua (glancing at Justen):

Congratulations.

Joshua (addressing the group):

All areas of this compound are now connected. Each of your private areas are accessible. You will find some additions. Now, you may all share Melissa's Olympic-sized pool. The outdoor garden has been extended to a field by a lake. You have one week to enjoy one another's company. Today is Monday. In seven days, we will meet again in the lounge area adjacent to this room. Everything will be revealed to you, and all your questions will be answered. Stage 2 Awareness will begin. For this entire week, I will not be available to anyone. You will find that all your immediate needs have been met. When we meet again, you will be given the knowledge that is required in order for you to decide your individual paths. To stay or to return. Enjoy these days, bond together, and relax. Until then, I bid you farewell.

Joshua turned and left. No one attempted to follow him, and no one commented on what they had just heard.

Emily:

After dinner, let's all go swimming!

Celeste:

> There's plenty of time for that later, not after we eat. I say we all curl up and watch a movie.

Jessica

> Okay!

And so it went. Just as Joshua had instructed. They enjoyed their time together as a group. Meals, movies, and long walks in the field with a view of the lake. Before dinner each night, the young ones went swimming in the pool, all under Celeste's watchful eye. She became like the *den mother* to them all. The group bonded. Melissa and Justen spent time together and became closer. When Celeste was not monitoring the young ones, she spent time with Barry. Emily was very good and prompt with orchestrating the young ones' preparation of all meals for the group: breakfast, lunch, and dinner.

She loved doing it, and everyone indulged her. She took notes on everyone's favorites and never failed to please. The group was comfortable, and everyone was in perfect health. As the week drew to an end, Melissa and Justen became more and more anxious. They wanted to know everything, yet they felt a weight bearing down on them … a sense of gloom. Something terribly important had brought them all together. They knew that each of them, in some profound way, had some part to play in the future of everyone else.

Chapter 8

Answers

8:38 a.m.

The day arrived. Joshua awoke the group according to their ages (oldest to youngest) at two-minute intervals. After the group freshened up and got dressed, Emily told them that she didn't feel like organizing breakfast. They each had the cold cereal of their choice with 2 percent milk. The young ones had orange juice; the adults, coffee. When they gathered their courage to go to the lounge (they did it together), Joshua was there waiting for them, sitting in an armchair. Joe Sample's *Ashes to Ashes* was playing faintly.

Barry thought:

Excellent choice. We're all going to burn today.

The young ones sat on the floor, on plush animal-shaped pillows. They gathered around Celeste (who had sunk herself deep into a huge beanbag). Barry sat upright in the La-Z-Boy ®, and Melissa and Justen sat together in the love seat, holding hands. The group positioned themselves to face Joshua.

Joshua (no longer wearing glasses or the trench coat):

Good day. I hope that all is well with each of you.

At any time while I am sharing with you that which you all need to know, so that each of you can decide on what you want to do, you may stop me to ask questions. Excuse yourself if you must for a refreshment or to gather your thoughts. I will wait and continue when we are all back together again.

No one spoke. Everyone seemed to be glued to their locations, apprehensive and somewhat afraid of what was to come.

Joshua:

As individuals and collectively, you have been very patient. Please allow me to apologize to each and every one of you for the ordeals that you have endured. The loved ones that you have been separated from and the loved ones that you have lost. None of your suffering has been by our doing. As you should now realize, we are here to help. As you learn, think of your time here and of what has been provided for you.

Melissa and Justen briefly looked at each other and squeezed each other's hands. Justen put his other arm around Melissa. Jessica abandoned her *zebra* and snuggled with Celeste in the beanbag.

Joshua:

Melissa, Celeste, Justen, and Barry, please bear with me, as what I am about to disclose to you all and the manner in which I speak will seem at times oversimplified. It is for the sake of the children. They too must reach a full understanding. Everything you are about to learn, unfortunately, is the truth about what is happening now and of what will transpire. That is, what will happen in the near future. From this point forward, all our conversations will be by talking or speaking out loud. We will no longer use telepathy to communicate—that is, through our minds. (pointing to his head) I will know all your thoughts; however, I will not share them with anyone, nor will I respond to them in any way.

Joshua (looking at Terrance, smiling and nodding):

You have done very well, Terrance. Thank you.

The room lights dimmed, and the music ended as a view screen descended from the ceiling, just behind Joshua.

Joshua:

Let us begin. This view screen will assist me as I help you to understand your reality.

You all, the others who were taken and the entire human race, are like children. For centuries—that is hundreds of years—your race has been exploring, learning, and growing. Along the way, they have comprehended—that is, they have learned—many things and have never learned many others. Some of your kind have developed behaviors that seek to destroy all of you.

The view screen illuminated, and the group sat and watched in silence and terror as various horrifying activities were displayed: murders, assaults, wars ... genocide. Nothing was censored; sound was included. The adults and the children were all able to see what mankind had become. They watched and knew the truth and gravity of Joshua's words.

Joshua:

Not only have you continually brought about needless—that is, without reason or cause—death to your own kind, but your actions are destroying this world. Natural resources are being depleted—that is, being used up—at an alarming rate, and wildlife in their natural habitats are virtually nonexistent. Forests and plants are being destroyed. Animals are losing their homes and have nowhere to live, let alone thrive. They only struggle to survive.

Your ozone layer and atmosphere, the protective shields that surround the earth, are slowly but steadily being polluted beyond repair. Worst of all, the proliferation and continued use of nuclear warheads on missiles and bombs and other weapons of mass destruction is at dangerous levels and is moving ever so close to the global annihilation of all life as you know it. Your planet is dying. We are here to help you avoid this ultimate disaster.

Tears began to fall softly from Emily's and Celeste's eyes. Barry's hands began to sweat and shake.

Joshua:

We are not of your world. We are travelers from a distant place. You may call us the Tarkum. We are many. We have been with you for a long time, studying, watching, and waiting until the time came for us to take action. That time is now. We have never interfered with your progress or lack thereof. Until now, we have only been silent observers. We want you to survive. That is the only reason why we are here. The other ones who were abducted, like yourselves, will assist us with our mission, if they so choose.

If we had not acted when we did, your civilization would have been doomed, destroyed by your own hand. Mankind would have ceased to exist.

Justen:

> Wait, how do you know that we won't change, that we can't change? How can you be so sure?

Melissa remembered how she reacted during her Stage 1 Awareness when Joshua explained her reality. She remembered the anger, the frustration, and the disbelief. She could sense those same feelings, those same emotions welling up in Justen.

Joshua:

What I am sharing with you is your reality. Humans are systematically destroying themselves and the planet Earth. After I have completed your Stage 2 Awareness, each of you will have a choice:

(1) To return to your lives with the knowledge you have of the Tarkum and of our mission but also knowing that you can never rejoin this group and our efforts. You will be fully aware what is to come and must accept that, at this point, it cannot be prevented.

You will live out the rest of your lives and die before the inevitable or perish in its wake.

(1) *You may choose to remain here with the Tarkum and participate, play an active role in what is the only hope, the only chance for the survival of the human race.*

As you know from your experience here, we of the Tarkum have special abilities that for now are above the limitations, comprehension, and understanding of your species. You know that we can heal your bodies, read your thoughts, and sustain your existence in complete comfort. We can also travel through the vast universe, space, at great distances and at great speeds. We can exist among the inhabitants of any occupied world without their knowledge and can assist mankind in starting anew. This is for those who are willing. It is only for those who wish to survive. Of the 650 individuals who were chosen, those who decide to remain here with us will enter into Stage 3 Awareness, from which there is no return. A chance to live on. An opportunity to continue to exist.

Melissa (as Justen kissed away the tears from her face):

> I don't know about the rest of you guys, but I need a break. Anybody up for some lunch?

Barry (standing up):

> I think it would be a good idea if we all took five or ten for some grub. What do ya say?

Everyone got up and headed for the kitchen. When they arrived, all their favorite dishes were waiting for them, prepared to perfection.

Emily:

> Hey! Don't take all the fun out of everything. Let us do something!

Joshua:

Today is a grave day for you all. Allow us to provide you with extra comfort.

Celeste:

> Okay, everybody, grab hands. Let us say grace, eat, get back to that dreaded den, and then let Joshua tell us the rest. We've all come this far.

And so it was. In whatever way they could, with such heavy thoughts on their minds, the group tried to enjoy their meals: Barry had grilled cheese, French onion soup, sweet tea, and some Wheat Thins; Justen had tuna fish on rye toast with chips and a Heineken; Melissa had a buffalo wing platter and some orange-pineapple juice; and Celeste had fettucine Alfredo with chicken and Welches grape juice.

The young ones shared some pizza with Hawaiian Punch, all except Terrance, who wasn't too hungry but did manage a bag of microwaved butter popcorn and a bottle of Fiji.

On this day, Joshua joined them, having a turkey cheeseburger and a bottle of root beer. An hour and a half later, they were back in the *room of gloom*, sitting in their same positions. This time, Barry reclined in the La-Z-Boy ®.

Joshua:

You are not alone in what you know as the world or the universe. There are star systems upon star systems with many inhabited planets and many other forms of intelligent life. Compared to human beings, some are more advanced in their existence; others are less.

The view screen illuminated again to show various civilizations throughout the universe, in their natural environments and in their natural forms. It was beautiful, simply breathtaking. The group was stunned.

Jessica (giggling):

Like *Star Wars*! But for real!

Joshua:

All life is connected.

As you know from your own experience with your own ecosystems here on Earth, the destructive behavior of one group of beings, namely humanity, affects all other groups. So is it with the universal fabric of life, which humans share with all life forms everywhere.

The view screen turned off and slowly retreated to the celling.

Our group, the Tarkum, have existed since the beginning, and we exist for only one purpose. That is to assist other intelligent life forms with their struggle for survival. We help to maintain the positive existence of the life force that connects and sustains us all. All though we have extensive abilities in the things that we are able to do, which seem extraordinary from your perspective, we do have limitations. Our charge and direction is clear. We cannot interfere with the natural progress of a group of beings. If self-destruction is imminent, then so be it. A species such as humanity, who has the responsibility of sustaining the life force of a world, must ultimately prove their ability to do so.

Terrance:

> So, if you know that someone is going to fall, you can be there to catch them, but you can't stop them from falling?

Joshua:

Not quite, Terrance. I will help you to understand. If we observe that a group of people are going to jump off a cliff to their doom, we can pick a few people out of the group before they all jump. We can then tell this select group of people about the pending jump and show them why they don't need to jump. We help them to develop a mind-set that will prevent them from joining that group in the first place, even though some of their friends, family, and loved ones are still a part of that doomed group. Then we offer them a choice:

(1) *Stay with us while the rest of the group jumps to their deaths.*
(2) *Rejoin the group, jump, and perish.*

Barry:

Wow, that's pretty bad. We don't stand a chance, do we? I mean, when you look at the big picture, we're pretty screwed, aren't we?

Joshua:

There is hope. That is why we are here. The Tarkum have traveled to many worlds and have observed the unfortunate self-destructive behaviors of countless species.

In our history, all of them to this very time, in your understanding would constitute millions of worlds. When we decide to act, it is only when we conclude that there is a chance for the survival of the species. We have never failed to save a group from the fate of so many others. That is, total self-annihilation.

The view screen behind Justen descended and was illuminated again.

Volcanic eruptions, tremors, earthquakes, tsunamis, hurricanes, and tornadoes notwithstanding, which are true natural disasters of this planet, many lives, human and otherwise, have been lost due to mankind's direct action or nonaction. Specifically, major forest fires, floods, the spread of deadly diseases, hunting to the point of near extinction of a species, wars upon wars upon wars, not to mention forced famine and genocide. Even with natural disasters, sufficient planning, paying attention to warning signs from the best scientific minds, and reduced development at the expenses of natural habitats would save millions of lives. We of the Tarkum are not here to pass judgment on your species. You have already set in motion that which has become your fate. You have created your own destiny.

In our observation, if we did not see a chance for the redemption of your species, we would have left you to your fate long ago—before the horrors of Auschwitz, Hiroshima, Nagasaki, the Twin Towers, and so many others of mankind's campaigns of death, destruction, and negligence.

Justen grimaced as images of the concentration camps, nuclear meltdowns, atomic explosions, war, destruction, fallout, acid rain, and crumbling skyscrapers flooded the view screen.

Joshua:

Celeste would have died with her precious Stacey in that plane crash, Barry would have succeeded in his attempt to kiss a cloud and would have fallen to his death, and Justen might have survived being shot twice, only to perish for certain in that medevac explosion. The children's charred remains would be scattered all over that hillside just outside of Norristown. You are all here together, right now in this place listening to me because we of the Tarkum believe that there is hope for your kind. No, we cannot prevent the terrible disaster that is to come by your own hand. However, we can help you, the chosen to survive it, thus ensuring the continued existence of the human race.

We want you to learn from the tragedy. We will help you understand and correct the behaviors in yourselves that would ultimately lead up to such calamity and utter destruction. We want to help you to not repeat the same mistakes that would begin another journey down that dark path. We have the desire and the means. We know exactly what we have to do. We have done this countless times before. We of the Tarkum have never failed. If each and every one of you decides to return to their lives, and that choice will be yours, then you will live out your existence and will die naturally or by some other means, or you will perish in the blast of a nuclear explosion or suffer slowly and die from one of the horrible conditions of its grim aftermath—that is, starvation or radiation poisoning. No life on Earth will survive.

There was silence for a full three minutes. No one spoke. Joshua waited for a question or response before he continued.

Justen:

You don't pull any punches, do you?

Joshua did not respond. Instead, the group heard a playback in the air of Justen's own words:

> Okay, Joshua, in very plain English, complete but to the point, I want to know everything—who you are, how and why I am here, where I am and what you want with me ... the truth and all of it, right here and right now.

Justen:

> Ouch. Didn't see that one coming.

Celeste (beginning to cry, thinking about Stacey):

> Why did you save us from our fates? Why us?

Joshua (in a warm and consoling tone of Voice):

You were not chosen at random. Of the billions of your kind, there is only a small percentage, a few who have the behavioral mind-sets to precipitate, cause, or set in motion such global death and destruction. The overwhelming majority of human kind is good, exhibiting nondestructive behaviors, positive and endearing characteristics. In our determination, we have selected the elite of your kind. You have all struggled most of your lives with extreme adversity and the evils of your world. Yet you have always remained committed to whatever you could do to help others and make the world a better place to live in.

It was not easy—and in most cases, it was very difficult—to be your very best and do the very best that you could. Even with the odds against your favor, you have persistently continued to try. Your true characters have always shown through for your loved ones and even perfect strangers. Your family was the human family. For reasons beyond your comprehension and understanding, our limit is always 650 entities out of billions per world, further subdivided into small groups such as yourselves. You and the others were chosen because, from our observations, you represent the very best of the best, the crème de la crème of the human race at this time. The individuals from the 650 who choose to remain with us and assist us in the rebuilding of this civilization after its eminent and almost total destruction represent the best chance for our success and the continued survival of your species.

Jessica:

> You're not human like us. What do you really look like?

Joshua:

Our true form is beyond your perception. To you, we would only be seen as light and energy.

In an instant, the entity that they all had come to know as Joshua transformed into a shapeless mass of yellow light and began floating around the room. It passed through walls, fixtures, furniture, and them. As it passed through each of them, they felt a warm, comfortable glowing sensation. The children giggled, and the adults smiled.

Joshua (returning to his human form):

Stage 2 Awareness is complete. You as a group have another week to enjoy one another's company again. Now you will be able to go outside. There are parks, cars for you to drive, and roads to drive them on. You will encounter animals of all kinds, and none of them will harm you in any way. You may approach and pet them as you see fit. The children will have bicycles, skateboards, and ponies to ride.

Melissa:

> But none of it will be real, right? I mean, what exactly is this place anyway?

Joshua:

You are correct, Melissa. All of this is a recreation taken from our knowledge of your world. The compositions of your comforts were taken from your own minds.

However, just as the food you have eaten and the beds you have slept in are real, so will everything else be. This place exits in a space outside of your world, and everything in it was created especially for you. I will return in seven days. At that time, I will meet separately with each and every one of you. We will talk, and you will tell me of your decision to stay or to return to your lives. Everyone must decide as individuals. Recordings are available of all Awareness Stages and of all your time here. In the library to your left, you may request any publication ever printed, any tweet or blog ever posted, watch any play, movie, or TV show ever performed or recorded. For you, Barry, that translates to every sporting event from every venue. Justen, the music repository is complete, from opera to classic rock. View screen systems are now available in your private rooms. I encourage each of you to indulge to your heart's content. The decision you have to make in a week's time will not be an easy one. You were all brought together in small groups as such to make this most difficult choice easier. I will be available to meet daily for one-hour sessions. With the children as a group at 1:30 p.m. after lunch, and with the adults as a group at 7:30 p.m. after dinner. For the sake of unity and transparency, participation is mandatory.

These meetings will be open forums for question and answers specifically related to information that was disclosed during Awareness Stages 1 and 2. There will be nothing revealed of Stage 3 Awareness. How we of the Tarkum plan to assist with the survival of the human race is knowledge only for those who choose to remain. Before I leave you, there is one more thing that you must know.

Another foreboding silence. Justen, Melissa, Barry, and Celeste all looked at one another. Barry, who had gotten up and was about to go for a spin in that vintage Lamborghini Diablo that he always wanted to own and that he knew was out there waiting for him (he was right), sat back down.

Justen thought:

> *What could it be now? What could be any worse than what we've just learned? We only have a week to digest all of this!*

Joshua:

Had the Tarkum not arrived to observe you once it became known that your species had embarked upon a path of self-destruction so many years ago, had we not selected 650 individuals from among you, in order to provide a base core to start anew and give the human race a chance at redemption, your species would have ceased to exist.

However, Earth would be restored; it would survive and continue to exist without you. Think of a family of seven who perish in a house fire because the father carelessly smokes in bed. After the funeral, the house would be restored, and another family would eventually move in. As part of the expansive web of life that extends beyond your galaxy, your home, planet Earth, is a crucial point. However, its current controlling inhabitants are not. Human beings have always been the caretakers of this world. In that capacity, as of late, they have failed in their duties and responsibilities. We of the Tarkum are here to help restore mankind to a status worthy of your charge and to avoid the alternative, which is to have another life form replace human beings and succeed where you have failed. Melissa, cancerous human cells must be removed from the body, as to not spread and infect healthy tissue, jeopardizing the life of the entire organism. Celeste, the Romeros of the world have to be caught and caged, as to not prey on innocent young females. Barry, if an investment analyst charged with managing a mutual fund portfolio continually loses position, that responsibility is removed from that individual, as to not risk further damage to the firm's value and reputation.

Justen, if any of the persons in that embassy room had posed a threat to your command, thus the survival of the group, your orders were to eliminate that threat with deadly force. It is also such with planet Earth. Its continued existence as a positive life force as a whole supersedes that of any of its inhabitants. If enough of you choose to remain, at least half to be exact, and that would be 325 individuals, then a second chance you will receive. A third you will not. If mankind starts down the dark path again, after your world has been restored, the human species will be eradicated and replaced as the guardians of Earth. Not by the Tarkum; that is not our charge. But rest assured, you will cease to exist. It will be as if you were never here at all. Ponder this also during this coming week.

And with that last somber note to add to the rest of the day's *good news,* Joshua took leave of them in human fashion, walking out of a front door and closing it behind him. Melissa and Justen took a spin on a Ducati Multistrada 1200 (something Melissa always wanted to do). Barry took the Lamborghini out for a stretch on a nearby Autobahn. Celeste piled the kids into a minivan, and they went for an afternoon cruise on a small sailboat on a nearby lake, accompanied by a couple of chimpanzees and some talking parakeets.

When they had all returned from their little excursions, their compound had been transformed into a luxurious replica of the Blandwood Mansion and Gardens in the Italianate style, complete with an outdoor pool, tennis and basketball courts to boot. The kitchen was fully equipped, and the pantry and freezers were fully stocked.

This week, there would be no magically prepared meals. Master Chef Emily was reborn. They now had two cats and a German shepherd, which Jessica named Simon, Pearly, and Max respectively. Justen called a meeting in the den before dinner.

Justen (addressing the group, even toned and serious):

> What we all are experiencing seems very unreal, like something out of a fairy tale. It may be hard to accept, but each and every one of us must find a way to embrace it as our reality. Joshua and the Tarkum he represents are real ... very real. Everything that we have seen and heard today about us, about human beings, about what we as a civilization have become is the absolute truth. Each of us, we have family and friends that we love, that we miss. Some are alive and safe for now, and some are not.

Justen (walking over to Celeste, taking her hand and kissing her on the forehead):

> But we are all here, right here, right now. Wherever this is, it doesn't matter.

> Like Joshua told us, what does matter is that we were chosen; we have a charge and a responsibility. I know that we all wish that we could bring our loved ones here with us. But we can't. I know that we wish that we could save everybody, but that's not the way it's going to be. In a week's time, when Joshua comes back, if you decide to go home—Melissa, I know you miss Michael, and I know that you want to see him again—but each of us should think of all of us as family now. There are 650 people if you believe what Joshua said, and I really do, who are just like us, who were chosen to make a difference. Somehow, someway with the help of the Tarkum, I believe that we can save humanity.

Justen (walking around the room and laying his hands on each one of their shoulders before returning to his seat):

> We can't undo the damage that has already been done, nor stop what is going to happen from happening, but we can survive it with Joshua's help. When we were being told everything today, I believed it, but I thought that if given the chance, knowing what I know now, I could go back and change people's minds.

> But then I realized that I've been thinking that my entire life. We can't stop it; it's too late for that. But don't you want to be a part of that new family, living in that better, rebuilt house, with the knowledge and understanding that not only do you not smoke in bed but that you don't smoke at all? I sure as hell want that chance. Do you? Let's eat.

Melissa embraced Justen. Their outing today was special—the cool fresh air, the intellectual one-on-one conversation about today's revelation and their pending decision. Throughout all her time here (wherever here was), her entire focus was: *do whatever you have to do to get back to Michael.* Now, she wasn't so sure.

Knowing what she knew, believing what she believed, just like Justen, could she really go back? Could she really just leave Justen and the others?

This and more she pondered along with the others who were trying to *sort things out* in their own minds, in their own way, for what would become the longest week in their entire lives.

Time

To live is to die.
To give is to get.
To laugh is to cry,
As to win is to bet.

To see is to hear.
To have is to need.
To love is to fear,
As to heal is to bleed.

To come is to go.
To sit is to walk.
To guess is to know,
As to sing is to talk.

We rise, and we fall.
We fight, and we lose.
We wait, and we call.
We touch, and we bruise.

We plot, and we scheme.
We choose, and we chase.
We dare, and we dream.
We reject and embrace.

We are, and we're not.
We attack and defend.
We bloom, and we rot.
When will it all end?

Barry and Celeste became lovers, as did Justen and Melissa. There were no complications ... no romantic courtships. The pure mental and physical attraction that existed between them was all that was needed. The gravity of their situation, their pending decisions, the imminent doom of mankind and the survival of its aftermath, none of these were contributing factors. It was an unadulterated, raw, and instinctive desire and need for each other, and so it was. It was beautiful, loving, caring, and blissful.

Barry came to Melissa on the second day after Joshua's revelation. She was sitting in the den watching *Rise of the Planet of the Apes,* trying to decide if this new series of movies would be as good as the first. Charlton Heston, Roddy McDowall—those stellar performances would be difficult to live up to.

Barry:

> You would pick a movie like this. What's wrong with you? Why aren't you watching *Miss Pettigrew Lives for a Day* or something like that?

Melissa laughed, paused the movie, stood up, and gave Barry a warm embrace.

Melissa:

> I don't know. It seems appropriate. You know, if we don't get our act together, we're out. They're in.

Barry:

How charming. Where's Justen?

Melissa:

Out on the Ducati. I can't get him away from that thing.

Barry:

Celeste and the kids went to the amusement park. They tried to drag me along, but I passed. Something about being the only souls there ... just wouldn't feel right. They plan to ride every roller coaster there, all twelve of them, twice.

Melissa:

She's great with them, they really love her.

Melissa could tell that something was on Barry's mind, but she waited until he felt comfortable enough to come out with it.

Barry:

Celeste and I were talking last night. (pausing) She's such an amazing woman, with all that she's been through, for her to be able to give so much love.

Melissa didn't respond, she let Barry continue.

Barry:

> I know that I have no right to say this to you, but on the other hand, I feel as though I have every right. Melissa, you have to stay. You can't go back.

Melissa:

> Barry, I—

Barry (interrupting her):

> Wait, I know. Michael ...

Melissa covered her mouth to hold back a slight gasp that would have surely been followed by a tear or two. Just the mention of his name, just the thought of seeing him again ...

Barry:

> Please come and sit down.

Grabbling her arm and shoulder with the gentlest of touch, he guided her to the couch, and they sat down together.

Barry (still holding Melissa):

> We need you—not just our group but the whole world, what will be left of it anyway, what it will be.

> They chose us Melissa, us ... all of us. Look at what they can do, what they've shown us. They didn't do this to us; no one did. We did this to ourselves. They're here, if you believe everything that Joshua has told us, and I believe that we all do, to save us, to give us all a second chance.

Melissa looked deep into Barry's eyes, into his soul, and what she saw was fear. She felt it. Barry let go of Melissa. He put his head in his hands for a minute, then looked up at her with teary red eyes.

Barry (in a shaky Voice):

> I'm scared, Melissa. I don't know if anyone else is, but I'm scared enough for all of us. What if we don't make it? What if we can't do it even with their help? It's going to be all on us. Joshua said they needed 325 out of 650 ... out of billions. What if too many people decide to go back? We need you; we all do. I'm not ready to check out like this, knowing that we have a chance do something about it.

It was never explained to Melissa in quite those terms. She began to listen, to really think hard about what Barry was saying.

Barry:

> Of all of us here in our group, you're the only one who left someone behind. Celeste and I, both of us left our people or were trying to before we were taken. Now we have each another. The children, they've always had each another, and they still do. Justen already left his people to try to save the world. Now, he has a real chance to do just that. To be cut off from your Michael, the way you were, after losing Stephen ...

Melissa wasn't mad. She took no offense to what Barry was saying, what he was trying to do. She understood.

Barry (after a brief pause):

> Celeste gave me orders to wait until she got back with the kids, so we could all try and persuade you together. I mean, who could resist a request from Jessica? But I couldn't wait. I had to try.

Melissa:

> I'll stay.

Now it was Barry who began to cry, heavy, heart-wrenching sobs that rocked his entire being, his very soul (again). Melissa put her arm around him and felt his desperation transform into pure joy.

Barry (when he could speak again):

> I just ... we ...

Melissa (putting her finger to Barry's lips):

> It's okay, it's okay. I know, I know ...

Melissa sighed.

> Every time one of my babies would leave me, a part of me would evaporate. To be able to save them, all of them, it's all I've ever wanted, ever dreamed about. Now, knowing that even if I go back to Michael, to the children, knowing that I won't be able to save them, any of them from what's going to happen, that changes everything.

What would I have to live for? What could I hope to strive for ... for them, for Michael, for myself? Now I have a chance to make a real difference. Barry, I feel it too. I've sensed it for a while now. After meeting you, Celeste, the children, after helping Justen through Stage 1 Awareness ...

Barry:

We were chosen for a reason, Melissa. If we can't do it together ...

Melissa:

Then we all cease to exist ... like we were never here.

They both looked away, a long pause ... silence. Each of them struggling with their own vision of what that meant. The thought of an entire civilization, their civilization, being eradicated, gone for all time ... never to return ...

Barry:

I don't want to go out like that.

Melissa:

We won't *(she stood up)*. We can't, we're going to do this.

Barry stood up, and they embraced again.

Barry (letting Melissa go, but still holding her hands):

You were easy.

Melissa (laughing):

Oh, was I now?

Barry:

A few tears here and there, like buttering a biscuit. I told Celeste I could do it. You know we're not done yet, right?

Melissa (laughing):

I know, I know.

Together:

Justen.

Melissa (with an anxious look on her face):

Even after that spiel he gave us at dinner the other night, he told me that he had changed his mind and was going back.

Barry:

> We caught him after he returned from an evening cruise last night, and he said to us: "I sure wish I could take this baby back with me. I'm going to have to work out something with Joshua. Man-o-man she's a beautiful beast!" trying to make it sound like a joke. But Justen doesn't joke. We knew that. We knew that he was trying to tell us without actually telling us that he was planning on going back.

At that moment, Celeste walked into the den and observed them talking, holding hands.

Celeste:

> What are you two up to? Can't turn my back for a minute.

Barry:

> Plotting, planning ... trying to decide on how we were going to off you and dispose of your body so that we could ride off into the sunset together.

Melissa:

> Listen to you. Now who has the dark mind?

Celeste walked over to Melissa and embraced her. She knew that Barry had been able to help change her mind.

Celeste:

> Thank you, thank you. It's going to be hard enough already, but without you, without all of us together. Now, on to the big mountain.

Celeste and Barry sat down on the couch, Melissa in the La-Z-Boy ®.

Melissa:

> He told me how he felt the day of the siege at the embassy, how he felt cheated and angry that the guerillas were about to blow his chance at trying to establish peace in the region, how it infuriated him. He said that even now, knowing what he knows and believing Joshua, a large part of him still feels that if given the chance, we could have saved ourselves.

Justen:

> And I still do.

Celeste, Barry, and Melissa turned as Justen entered the den. Walking over to Melissa, he pulled her up, kissed her, sat down in the La-Z-Boy ®, and pulled her down to sit in his lap.

Justen:

> I was going back but not for that reason. I know now that our destiny is sealed. The evil is too deep rooted.

Melissa (confused):

> But you said that you were going back anyway, that part of you still wanted to try to complete your mission?

Justen:

> As most adults of our species do, I lied. I was going back but not for that reason. I was only going back because now I know what's really important, at least to me anyway. No matter what, here, there, in the future, whatever, whenever … I'm not going to be anywhere without you, my sweet.

Celeste grabbed Barry's hand and squeezed it tight.

Justen (after kissing Melissa's hand):

> I thanked the Lord after I realized, after I accepted Joshua's revelation. I mean, come on, to be chosen to jump-start this thing, do it all over again the right way? It was a G-d send. There was no way I was going back. But after us, it didn't matter. I didn't care. Whatever happens, happens. If you were going back because of Michael, then I was going with you. It's selfish, I know. It's probably wrong, knowing all this. But, baby, you're stuck with me. If you're staying, I'm staying.

Melissa (starting to cry again):

> I'm not going to lie to you, Justen. I love you. I really do, with all my heart. But even after us, after all this, I was going back. I just had to see my boy again.

Getting up off Justen's lap, Melissa went over to Barry, who stood up. They embraced again.

Melissa (still holding Barry tightly):

> But Barry, my dear, dear Barry ...

Celeste covered her mouth with both hands and began to sob.

Melissa:

> Your words somehow reached deep down inside of me and laid bare the selfishness rooted in my desire to get back to Michael.

Barry:

> Melissa don't, you don't have to ...

Melissa (letting go of Barry):

> No, it must be said. You were so right. We were all chosen. We have to try. We have to. Your pain, your fear is all our fears.

Celeste got up and went over to embrace Melissa. They cried together.

Celeste:

> My Stacey, even deep down inside, my Milton at one point, they meant so much to me, but this ... wow ... this is a lot. I don't know how we can do it. But I know that if anybody can, we can. The children, Jessica, (another tear or two escapes) my G-d—have you ever known someone so pure, so beautiful? It's hard to believe that any of these children are from the same world, our world.

Melissa:

> We're going to have to draw from their strength. They're going to sustain us all.

Barry:

> Six hundred and fifty. Joshua said that some may even go back. But those that hang in there, if we have enough, if they're anything like this group, then we got a real shot. I feel good about our chances.

Everyone smiled.

Justen:

> This week was for us. Those kids, they had it all figured out a long time ago. It was probably a no-brainer for them. Just another adventure, another set of skits to save the world.
> They were already a group with a mission. Now they're on Broadway.

As things turned out, Melissa wasn't that hard of a sell, Barry's truthfulness, his rawness was all that she needed to hear, like a shot of adrenaline. Justen was even easier. To have the love of someone like Melissa?

How could any being ... from any world, any man ... from any time, have that and then just leave it? Walk away from it willfully? He wasn't built like that. He wasn't Justen of the Tarkum; he was Justen from Earth, and no power anywhere could persuade him to leave her side.

Chapter 9

Rebirth

8:40 a.m.

When Joshua knew that they all had decided to stay, he didn't wait for the week to end. He knew because their thoughts were his to know. He came to them during breakfast the next day when they were all together, before they went their separate ways for the day's adventures. He came through the doorway as if he had been in the den.

Joshua:

Congratulations. You have all decided to stay.
Stage 3 Awareness begins now.

Barry:

> Wow. You don't waste any time, do you?
> What happened to our week of peace?

Joshua:

Collectively, if you would like the remaining four days to relax and enjoy your comforts, then it will be granted.

Celeste:

> Shut up, Barry. Finish your French toast and let the man speak. Don't you think we've waited long enough?

Jessica triggered giggles from the young ones.

Barry:

> Yes ma'am.

Melissa looked over at Justen, who wasn't smiling at all. He just had a grave look on his face.

Joshua (looking at Justen):

Of all the 650 individuals, you were taken last. There has been a time lapse since your medevac was obliterated by a surface-to-air missile of exactly ten years, one month, and three days. In order to prepare you for what you must face, you must watch the events as they unfolded.

Your world has already been destroyed.

Very little significant life remains. What does will not survive much longer. You will observe how the missiles with nuclear warheads were launched.

You must witness how the targeted major cities were all destroyed, one by one. You must see how your people have perished. It is horrible to watch, but you must know everything. In order to fully prepare your minds for what lies ahead, you must feel in your hearts and souls that which should never be felt ever again. You have been chosen. We of the Tarkum will guide you, and together we will succeed. But first, it begins by watching the end. Please, finish your breakfast and join me in the den.

Melissa (crying softly):

> You knew all this time? You knew that we could never go back? That there is nothing left to go back to? Why? Why did you have us believe that we had a choice? Michael, everyone ... they're all gone?

Joshua:

Yes, Melissa, that is correct. However, the deception was necessary. The illusion was with purpose. Your kind, especially the female gender, is a highly emotional species, extremely susceptible to the adverse effects of shock. Remember how you reacted during your Stage 1 Awareness. How you resisted the revelation of your reality.

Your thoughts were also known to us. It was the same for many of the adults in the pool of 650 individuals. To disclose to the collective the harsh realities of what has transpired, without the healing buffers of time and gradual understanding by way of the Awareness Stages, would have damaged your spirits too deeply. It would have put our mission at risk. We cannot fail. You will succeed. Only the children, all the children, were capable of accepting the truth immediately. However, the children need your guidance as much as you need their strength and ability to accept reality.

Celeste:

> Thank you, Joshua. I know what you did, how you did it was for the best. I certainly needed the time and all of this to help me adjust. I'm still not all the way there yet.

Deep down, Melissa knew it too. They all did. The young ones processed this revelation with a sense of relief. They accepted it as an end to the nightmare. The continued, never-ending manifestations of their adult counterparts' capacity to do evil was finally over. To have everything gone, with a chance to start over, was to them the best worst thing that could have happened.

Celeste (glancing at Melissa):

> I'm not completely, fully at peace yet with losing Stacey, losing everything the way that things happened, but without the experience of what you have provided for us and the way that you brought us all together, I probably wouldn't have made it this far.

Melissa (with a slight touch of sarcasm):

> Well, hip-hip-hooray! Excuse me. I have to leave this party to be alone for a minute—you know, because of my frailness and all. If I stay in this room another second, I might just crumble up and turn to dust. Then you'd only have 649, but you probably would be better off. I mean, what good am I? Who needs a weak, pathetic, whimpering little creature like me at a time like this? Right?

Melissa got up, left, and went to her room. There, she lay down after closing and locking the door (which didn't have a lock on it until just now). With her head buried deep in her pillow, she sobbed. No one tried to stop her. No one got up to go and comfort her. They just let it be.

Justen:

> What if? What if any one of us would have decided to go back? What would have happened then? Would we have slipped into a coma and just never woken up? A series of Tarkum-induced mercy killings?

Joshua:

Pease try to understand, Justen. We of the Tarkum are not like humans. Our kind is of a different essence. In terms that you would understand, our composition is only that of caring and compassion. Only of love. We are incapable of inflicting cruelty, pain, or suffering on any life form. We have abilities far beyond your comprehension. In selecting the 650 entities to assist us in our mission, we are able to calculate and project with absolute certainty all possible scenarios for an individual's reaction to any given situation. If there was anything less than a 100 percent probability that the choice would be to remain, that entity was not selected. The possibility of reducing the quota of 650 never existed. Even with this knowledge, the process required that you were presented with the choice and allowed to reach this decision without interference.

The illusion of needing only 325 to remain of the selected 650 was, again, part of our process to prepare you for your charge. Strength in numbers remains one of your strongest concepts of the best way to achieve the objective of any mission. Our plan is flawless. Earth will be restored, and humans will remain as its caretakers for a much-deserved second chance at survival. You will succeed. We have never failed.

Joshua waited for a moment to see if anyone else had a question, comment, concern, or statement to make. None came.

Take as much time as you need. I will begin when we are all together in the den.

Joshua didn't get up and walk into the den, nor did he transform into a yellow ball of light energy and float over to the den. He was just there; then he wasn't.

To the group, it was like waking up from a dream. The group finished eating, and Celeste escorted the young ones to the den. The men washed the dishes and cleaned up the kitchen.

Barry:

> So, this is it, huh? We're in it for the long haul.

Justen:

> Looks like it. Damn it! Got to give it to Joshua and his crew; they run a smooth game.

Barry:

> I'm not so sure about their selection process though. I mean, look at me. Cream of the crop? Top of the line and all that? I don't think so. I was calling it quits, about to check out before the real crap hit the fan. I had given up, man.

Justen (extending his hand):

> Haven't you figured out yet that you can't under estimate these guys? They know exactly what they're doing. No matter what, you were chosen, Barry. Just like the rest of us. You're here because you belong here. Think of all the people you helped with your secret donations. Everything you struggled for, earned ... you just gave it away without hesitation. How many people could have done that? You're made of the right stuff Barry, I'm glad you're here.

Barry gripped Justen's hand, and they locked in an arm hug.

Barry:

> Thanks, man. Thanks. Coming from you, it means a lot.

They finished cleaning up and joined the others in the den. Melissa was already there.

She went to Justen and embraced him.

Melissa:

> I'm okay. I'm okay. I know that they were right. No more illusions now. No more games. We've got our work cut out for us. Let's do this.

The groups settled into their favorite positions.

Joshua:

It is time for you to meet the others. But first, we will proceed with your first lesson. Children, sit on the couch. Emily, Terrance, Jessica, and Brandon, in that order. Justen, sit on the floor in the beanbag alone. Barry and Melissa, sit on the love seat. Celeste, sit upright in the La-Z-Boy ®. Humans are used to operating within their comfort zone. You must begin to change this behavior and embrace things that are different. You must endeavor to seek it out whenever, wherever possible.

The more you find yourselves having to operate with unfamiliarity—that is, things that you are not used to—the better you will become at it. One of the major flaws of the past society that we observed was its inability to accept and embrace differences, without judgment and exclusion. Not just tolerance but complete acceptance. This has been the basis for shunning someone from being included in a work office club, not playing with certain kids who may be different in some way from the majority of the group, mass murder, and racial cleansing. Not a pack of Raisinets ® that are all the same but a bag of plain and peanut M&Ms ® mixed together, different colors and different fillings. The example is oversimplified, even for the children, but is a base example of a very important fundamental concept that must permeate the thought process of all. Your history is full of writings from individuals who have identified all that you need to know in order to survive and thrive in peace. The human race must learn to accept and practice all that is for the good of mankind and to reject all that is not. We of the Tarkum will guide you on how to inherently make this a continued part of your existence.

At no time during this Stage 3 Awareness is anyone allowed to move from their designated locations until otherwise instructed. Justen and Melissa, do not seek each other out.

Barry and Celeste, please remain apart. Jessica, if needed, you may find comfort in Terrance or Brandon. Do not go to Celeste.

The lights dimmed, and the view screen descended and illuminated, showing a group from a different region, changing at two-and-a-half-minute intervals. Although the 650 individuals were from all the 195 nations on Earth, no country, region, or geographic location identifiers of any kind appeared. Just one group ... the human race. There was conversation, laughter, and joy. The Tarkum interceded with universal translators so that all could speak and be understood in their native language.

The sheer knowledge shared by everyone that they were all that remained of mankind united them in a special way. It helped to form a strong, universal bond that transcended distance. The technical gathering lasted for a little over an hour. After each group had the opportunity to see all their counterparts, the view screens went dark.

Joshua:

Please partake of beverages and snacks of nuts, berries, and fruits in the dining areas. Use the restrooms and then return to your designated areas. I will continue once all are present.

Breaks were taken, and the lovers snuck in a few kisses and hugs.

Barry:

> This isn't going to be as bad as I thought. I'm having fun already!

Celeste:

> Check back in when you have to start plowing fields and planting crops. Then let me know if you're still having fun.

Barry:

> As long as I know that I'm coming home to your sweet stuff, I'll plow and plant all day, smiling and grinning all the way!

Melissa:

> You two are a mess.

Barry:

> Don't front. I saw you and Justen in the hallway. It's all good. Love makes the world go around! Ain't that right, Justen?

He received a smile but no verbal response. Everyone settled down in their places as instructed.

Joshua:

Everyone knows me. Although you call me by different names and have encountered me at different times in your lives and even now in your respective spaces and locations, I am only one entity. We of the Tarkum have the ability to bend time and space. We only do so for your convenience. Each of us, of my kind, is charged with the salvation of one species at a time. Earth, the human race, is my responsibility. My current charge. My current challenge. Will you all help me to succeed?

Clapping, cheering, whistling, and the shouting of "Yes!" in all languages was audible to everyone. This time, voices were heard in their respective tongues.

Joshua, I love you!

Thank you … thank you!

Joshua (smiling at everyone, everywhere):

Very well. You are all too kind. I will do what I am allowed to do. To help you to rebuild. To start anew. Your task is great. I am confident, however, that you will succeed. But first, you must all witness the end.

A moment of somber silence for all followed.

Joshua:

We have no desire to cause pain. You have experienced enough grief and despair to last a thousand lifetimes. However, this new beginning must be grounded in the reality and knowledge of what was. I will display the key points and narrate what you need to understand. At any time, from anyone, anywhere, please stop me with questions or the need for more clarification on any point. I will explain.

The global *dens* dimmed, and the view screens illuminated to display the situation room of the Israeli government. It had been a little over one month since Justen's medevac was destroyed. For fear of retaliation, no militant group ever claimed responsibility for the attack. The Israeli people were restless.

They were more afraid than they had ever been. They had accepted the reality that most nations in their region refused to accept their existence.

They had accepted and prepared themselves for the harsh reality of suicide cars, buses, and human bombers, repeated grenade and rocket launches on settlements, border patrol skirmishes, and endless waves of anti-Semitic propaganda in all venues, publications, and media forms.

They vowed as a nation to always protect their citizens and to continually fight for their G-d-given right to exist.

But a nuclear Iran?

From the moment that the possibility became a gruesome confirmed reality, the military leaders knew what had to be done. Unlike the US and 9/11, they were not going to wait until disaster struck to react. They were going to be proactive. A first strike? Not exactly. More like an assassination of a missile base. They plotted, and they planned. With or without the help of the US or any Islamic so-called ally, they were going to defuse the situation—by any means necessary.

In theory, the plan was simple. But logistically, it would be difficult to design and carry out.

The goal was to disarm the Iranian nuclear threat immediately and permanently. Israel, a nation that since its charter was established and its sovereignty was ratified in the UN Counsel had been on the defensive, was about to go on the offensive.

All options were discussed, from a covert operation to a full-scale declaration of war. Nothing was overlooked. What was agreed upon was a silent campaign. Its objective was to get in, disarm, and get out. Straight to the point.

Cut to the chase.

The mission was well conceived and well designed.

The US and Saudi Arabia (who still felt embarrassed that the vice president of the United States of America was almost killed on their watch) assisted in the final planning and in the execution of the operation. An Israeli team of nuclear experts was smuggled into Iran, and before anyone knew what was happening, the team was looking at the control mechanism of not only a nuclear warhead but a nuclear warhead attached to an ICBM.

It was fully functional and fueled. An examination of the guidance system revealed that it was targeted for Tel-Aviv. The disarmament commenced, but the Iranians had installed a failsafe. As soon as the first wire was cut, somehow the missile launch countdown timer was triggered ... sixty seconds. The ICBM was hot.

Of all the nuclear nations, none of them (not even the Soviet Union or China) had installed failsafe timers on ICBM missile launch systems equipped with nuclear warheads. This was dangerously ludicrous, completely unexpected, and typical of the mind-set of the radical Iranian leadership at the time.

This is exactly what all the nations of Earth had feared—a terrible weapon of unimaginable mass destruction under the control of crazy idiots with reckless irresponsibility.

A failsafe timer on an ICBM launch system attached to a functional nuclear warhead!?

Fools. Anything could go wrong. Accidents did happen! Oh well, too bad, so sad ... for Israel and everyone else. There was no time to defuse it. Calls were made to scramble some Israeli Boeing F-15 Eagles to blow it out of the sky once the doomsday launch occurred. But there was no time to locate, arm, and get the jets in range. A complete evacuation was impossible, given the missile's flight time of a little over an hour to traverse approximately 1,400 miles. And it didn't matter anyway; this was a nuclear missile!

30 seconds .. 10 .. 9 .. 8 .. 7 .. 6 .. 5 .. 4 .. 3 .. 2 .. 1

The missile launched. Tel-Aviv and the surrounding area of Israel was obliterated. Another nuclear holocaust, this time conceived by Iran but triggered by Israel's own hand (however accidently, in an attempt to save lives).

Barry gripped Melissa's wrist so tightly as they watched the force of the nuclear explosion she thought her bones would shatter. But she didn't try to get him to let go. Jessica and Emily cried; Terrance and Brandon comforted. Celeste sat in shock, with both hands covering her mouth.

Justen hung his head in shame. But it wasn't over. The worst was yet to come. The nuclear blast was so powerful that it generated a supersonic shockwave that was received by satellite receptors passing within range of Tel-Aviv. The signal was relayed and misinterpreted by hundreds of missile defense systems orbiting the globe as a hostile attack.

Technological achievements, which had become the focal point of some of mankind's greatest accomplishments, was so too the author of its pending destruction. The group watched in horror as a multitude of counterstrike nuclear missiles were launched. Each projectile targeted a different city, a different nation ... our enemy.

The missiles on nuclear subs did not launch. The erroneous signal did not penetrate the deep waters of the oceans. One by one, the bombs fell, destroying city after city, nation after nation. Kiev, Moscow, Washington D.C., Pyongyang, London, Ankara, Beijing, Minsk ... and many, many more. The people perished. Of the 193 nations of earth, none were spared. All in all, 9,220 nuclear missiles were launched with their deadly payload. Several of the missiles missed their targets and detonated in volcanos and on major underground faults. This triggered eruptions, earthquakes, and tsunamis. There were floods and lava landslides, which precipitated massive fires.

The devastation was unlike that of any fictional feature film ever produced that projected doom, destruction, and disaster. The Dwayne Johnson thriller *San Andreas* was, by comparison, an animated cartoon. This was all too real.

Joshua did not spare any footage of the atrocities; the 650 witnessed it all. After a while, no one cried. All that remained was a deep sense of appreciation that they were still alive, that they had been spared. There was still more. After the mushroom clouds had subsided, the nuclear ash descended, and the deadly radiation that followed poisoned all that had survived (bacteria and fungi included). Life on planet Earth ceased to exist, leaving in its wake a barren wasteland.

The view screens did not go dark and ascend into the ceiling; they simply vanished as the lights returned to normal.

Joshua:

Please take this time to indulge in any comforts as needed. This includes nourishment, relaxation, video, audio, exercise, brief excursions, and intimacies as so desired. We will continue Stage 3 Awareness back here in the den in exactly three hours. There will be no more restrictions as to where you must sit. Please be prompt.

Everyone looked at their wrists to find exquisite gold and diamond watches with leather bands, set at 1:00 p.m.

Joshua:

Please accept these timepieces as special gifts from us to you. They will illuminate five minutes before attendance is required for any special meeting. They also glow in the dark, and your names are engraved on the back. The clock face displays a rotating hologram of the planet Earth orbiting your primary star, or as you know it, the sun.

Melissa:

These are absolutely beautiful.

Justen (grabbing Melissa's hand and leading her away):

Not as beautiful as you. Come with me and let me tell you all about it.

Everyone went off to do their thing. At exactly five minutes to three, everyone's watches began to glow and gently vibrate for ten seconds. The group reconvened in the den, and Joshua was there waiting for them. Gone were the plush pillows, the beanbag, the lone La-Z-Boy ®, the couch, and the love seat. Joshua stood in the center of the room surrounded by several La-Z-Boy ® rocker-recliners, on coasters for easy movement. One for each of them.

Joshua:

Welcome back to you all. Please gather around me and be seated. The worst is over. Now humanity can move forward to an existence of peace and prosperity. Although we of the Tarkum have the power to expedite the healing of your planet, it has been a standing practice of ours to allow for ten years to pass before the process can commence. Our conversations in reference to time during your Stage 1 Awareness were not deceptions.

Your very last sleep was for a decade. What you recall as a good night's rest was actually ten years in stasis. Everyone was only awakened this morning. Now, you must sleep again. We must prepare your planet for you to re-inhabit it. For that to occur, we must use all our energy. To maintain all your comfort areas, the habitat, surroundings, lakes, landscapes, forests, wildlife, and to provide you with nourishment is a considerable drain on our resources. It is time. You must say your farewells for now and return to your rooms. For the last time, you will all be put into stasis for a period of one year. When you awaken, you will no longer be here but on your restored planet. Each of you will be as you are now, unchanged, in perfect health, and with all your memories. Nothing will remain of your previous civilization. You must rebuild again. We of the Tarkum will be there to assist you. Please accept our apologies, Justen and Barry; the Ducati and Lamborghini will not be there with you. Of the 650, there are engineers, doctors, scientists, mathematicians, and teachers. Collectively, you have retained your cumulative knowledge of the wealth of positive achievements that is the legacy of your predecessors. Even your knowledge of the power to destroy. However, if you choose to use it, if you decide to go down the dark path of destruction again, you will do so alone.

We of the Tarkum will not be there to assist you. It is time to sleep.

Peace be unto you, and I bid you farewell.

That valediction was heard in each of their minds as the vaguely familiar, somewhat soothing Voice they had all come to know and cherish. The essence that was Joshua of the Tarkum transformed into a bright yellow ball of light and energy and slowly dissipated.

Everyone stood up and hugged everyone else. Tears of happiness, joy, and hope flowed again as they shared a group hug. Celeste escorted the young ones to bed, accompanied by Barry. One by one, they were hugged again, kissed, and tucked in.

Jessica (to Celeste):

> When I wake up, I want to be with you.

Celeste (holding back her tears):

> I'll never leave you. I'll be with you forever.

Celeste and Barry turned off the light, left Jessica's room, and closed the door. Back in the den, they were greeted by Justen and Melissa.

Melissa (smiling):

> All right, you two. Straight to sleep and no funny business.

Barry (looking at Celeste):

> After all this, are you kidding me? I'm going to lie down beside her and hold her like there's no tomorrow ... even though I know that there is.

Another round of warm embraces. Barry and Celeste headed for the pillows and sheets. As soon as they were gone, Joshua reappeared.

Melissa stepped away from Justen.

Joshua (addressing Justen):

You will not be sleeping with the others.

Justen looked at Melissa, who just stood there smiling, not showing any signs of despair.

Melissa:

> It's okay, my sweet. I already know.

Joshua (addressing Justen):

You have been chosen. You will no longer be Justen of Earth. You will become Justen of the Tarkum. Your essence is unique. Your desire to save your fellow humans has been the strongest of the 650. You must accept our offer so that you may assist us in saving countless other species from the doom and desolation that mankind has endured. It is your true calling.

Justen (looking at Melissa):

> I can't leave you. As much as want to do this, I can't be without you.

Joshua:

And you won't have to. As you develop your abilities, as you learn how to harness your power, you will no longer be bound by the boundaries of time and space. They will become yours to bend at your will. You can be with Melissa whenever there is a mutual desire. But first, you must learn.

Melissa:

> Head on out, trooper, but don't take too long. I saw some nice hunks in the 650. A girl can't wait but for so long you know.

Joshua:

Do you accept?

Justen (smiling, glowing):

> Oh, don't you worry, baby. I got this.
> When you wake up, I'll be right there.
> Come on, man. Let's do this.

Melissa watched as Joshua and Justen transformed into bright balls of yellow light. They hovered in the air for a minute or two, then slowly faded into nothingness. In her bed on her way to sleep, she smiled. Unbeknownst to the others, during the moments when she retired to her room after learning that Earth had already been destroyed, Joshua allowed Melissa to travel back through time.

He allowed her to spend ten years with Michael. From age six to sixteen, she was with him. Joshua explained to her that this opportunity to spend time with her son was not without condition. She had been chosen. She was part of the 650 and had to return. To Michael, she would develop and succumb to non-Hodgkin's lymphoma (just like Alicyn). Melissa knew the parameters and accepted. Melissa also knew that somehow, someway, Justen of the Tarkum would keep his promise. And so it was.

Justen (of the Tarkum):

Wake up, Melissa, my sweet. Wake up.

Epilogue

Humanity has evolved as the epitome of excellence as the caretakers of a world. Balance has been restored, and the inhabitant species exist in a harmonious state that enriches the ecosystem and the quality of life for all. The Tarkum have ceased monitoring, but they invite potential caretakers and those who were given a second chance to come, witness, study, and attempt to emulate life as it exists on Earth (*Species Observation*). Melissa, Celeste, Barry, and the young ones (Terrance, Jessica, Brandon, and Emily), along with Joshua and Justen of the Tarkum and the other individuals who comprised the original 650, were more than successful.

After the bombs fell, after the radiation reduced the remaining remnants of life on Earth to dust, they were able to rebuild, to start anew. It has been seven hundred years, and Earth exists as the jewel of the universe. It has become a light of life that shines brightly across the galaxies. War, disease, poverty, hatred, neglect, oppression, abuse, despair, and desperation exist only in the archives—realities of a civilization long since removed, never to return. In their place exist pure love, nurturing, caring, and efforts to increase the sustainability and quality of all life.

The entity that is Joshua of the Tarkum has been reassigned to a world at the edge of the galaxy, to begin a new watch, waiting to initiate the abduction process for a new set of 650 entities on a planet on a path to attempted destruction. Calculating the right time to insert himself into their lives, at key intervals ... moments of despair. To be that reassuring thought, that comforting Voice, for this world has begun its own *descent into maelstrom*. The Tarkum have determined (for it is their decision to make) that this species deserves a second chance. The Mukrat are on standby ...

The entity that is Justen of the Tarkum has mastered all special techniques and has added his own uniqueness from his existence as Justen of Earth to his abilities. It was Justen of the Tarkum who initiated the *Species Observation* system. He also has been assigned to other worlds and has selected the 650 for his current charge ... the abductions have begun.

Justen of the Tarkum has done well. He has assisted in the salvation of 312 species since Earth. However, even with the prospect of timeless missions of mercy as a member of the Tarkum life force, for him, a new overwhelming desire has emerged. It is the product of a blend. The composition of his essence as Justen of Earth and of the Tarkum has prioritized for him a new goal in his mandate to maintain the fabric of life, and that is to eliminate the need for the Mukrat to exist ... forever.

All species throughout the connected web of life must exist to promote what is positive, enriching, and nurturing for all other life—a constant cycle of productive energy, forever growing, recycling. The essence of sustainability. The entity that is Justen of the Tarkum will find a way, for it is his true belief that somehow, someway, the darkness can be removed for all time—the darkness that precipitates the need for the Mukrat.

There is no warning. They appear out of thin air. A hovering ball of crimson light and energy, with no apparent shape or form, effortlessly gliding toward its intended target ... reaching its destination, immobilizing, engulfing, paralyzing. Slowly, methodically, the life force within is drained, depleted, like air escaping from a balloon but with no sound. In a matter of minutes, all that remains is a withered shell.

Needing only moments to compact and store the life energy into its reserves, the collector turns bright blue, then back to crimson again, and in an instant, it returns to the nothingness from which it came. This process is repeated everywhere, anywhere, wherever life of any significance exists. They are the collectors. There is no defense, no escape. They are not affected or deterred by any action. All matter and negative energy directed toward them passes right through them. They have but one purpose—to drain all life force from a planetoid, to compact, store, and be released at a later time as pure, recycled positive energy for the purpose of growth and regeneration.

They are not dreaded or feared, for they are unknown. They do not exist ... until they exist. They are, and then they're not. They are the Mukrat. Their presence signals the end for the inhabitants of a doomed world, which is often a multitude of species. The planetoid must be restored. The caretakers of a world are given the charge, assigned the task to enrich, sustain, and protect, to foster coexistence in harmony for the greater good of all life. This dominant species is given this chance and is allowed to fail once ... sometimes not at all.

Planetoids have resiliency beyond the scope and comprehension of the species that are its inhabitants. Collectively, or as individual groups, they do not have the capacity for total destruction of the world or all the life in it. They can only demonstrate this intent via purpose or as a side effect of negligence. In its early stages, this draws the attention of the watchers ... the Tarkum. They are allowed to continue down their path and reach their destination of destruction ... once. If it is determined that a second chance is warranted, a select few (by comparison) are chosen—always 650 entities in total, the very best of the best, the crème de la crème at the time. If this is the will of the anti-Mukrat, the Tarkum (the entities charged with species preservation where possible), the global annihilation of life is allowed to occur. The chosen ones are removed and protected from the fate of their kind.

They are given assistance, a chance to rebuild anew, to remain as caretakers of the world.

This can begin only after the planetoid has had a chance to heal—naturally in part and with the assistance of the Tarkum to help neutralize the deadly effects of radiation or a similar poison. All destructive energy must be completely dissipated. The chosen of the dominant species are returned, but they are watched carefully. The Mukrat are there, and then they are not. Their actions and activities are constantly analyzed. If it is determined that history is attempting to repeat itself, the crimson balls of light and energy begin to appear.

Such is the charge of the Mukrat. All significant forms of life undergo a metamorphosis from the present state, compacted and stored to be released at a later time—crimson to bright blue to crimson again. For the resiliency of a planetoid cannot withstand a second attempt at total destruction. This must be avoided, will be prevented, and cannot be allowed to happen. The Tarkum and the Mukrat exist as the essence of sustainability. They are born out of the very fabric of life itself, protecting the very nature of life, ensuring that the balance of life remains and is sustained everywhere where life exits.

Justen of the Tarkum,

Your task lies before you . . .

Worlds await.

About the Author

Maurice E. Kennedy, Jr. is a native of Philadelphia, Pennsylvania. He lives with his wife of ten years, Marie; his two sons, Errol and Bret; and two cats in Germantown. He grew up in a strong family with his father, Maurice Sr.; mother, Sarah; older sister, Antoinette; and two younger sisters, Tammy and Miriam. He maintains a close relationship with his baby sister, Miriam (his heart), and her husband, Marc, one of the "Beamer-Boys."

After completing his studies in computer science at the Hospital of University of Pennsylvania in 1984, Mr. Kennedy went on to build an extensive thirty-five year career as a senior computer programmer analyst and instructor. *The Voice* is permeated with his real-life experiences, and although is not meant to be perceived as an inspirational work, the themes of love, harmony, and peaceful coexistence do reflect some of the values that he holds dear.

His two primary inspirations for writing came from Dr. Rudolph R. Windsor, author of *From Babylon to Timbuktu* and other books (and a true mentor and friend), and from a poetry class he took at Temple University/ PASCEP (where he has taught for more than twenty-five years) with Dr. Regina Jennings, who teaches African American literature at Rutgers University and is the author of *Midnight Morning Musings: Poems of an African American*.

Although *The Voice* is a work of fiction, it is Mr. Kennedy's hope that readers can relate to the characters, find the story line interesting, and take away something positive from the novel. Other publications by the author include *Developing Dynamic Databases, Creating Professional Spreadsheets, The Art of Chess,* and *In Essence* (a poetry collection).

For more information about the author, please visit https://sites.google.com/site/mkenterprisesdpp/.

For questions or comments about *The Voice,* please email the author at mekjspa.development@gmail.com.

Printed in the United States
By Bookmasters